LUST

LOLA TAYLOR

A WOLF WHO HAS SPENT HIS LIFE IN THE SHADOWS OF HIS PAST...

Beta werewolf—and ex–bounty hunter—Shadow knew when his Alpha commanded—er, "politely growled"—for him to attend the werewolf summit, that it was going to royally suck. Not only does he not want to fool around with all that royal werewolf bullshit, but he also knows he's not exactly everybody's favorite guy. Considering he ruined a lot of those werewolves' lives in his old profession, he'll be lucky if he can survive the weekend. Not to mention his mating Fever is driving him insane—and so is the feisty Alpha female he's Marked as his mate.

A QUEEN OF WOLVES WHOSE REIGN IS THREATENED...

Spirited Breanna Whiteclaw is barely holding it together. With an ornery Alpha named Strider out to make her—and her pack—his own, and with her pack recovering from recent attacks by an unknown enemy, she has her paws full. Attending the summit means leaving her pack in their time of need, but as a royal werewolf, she knows she has no choice. Add to that the fact that her Blood Moon is approaching, and she has yet to find a mate—until the devilishly handsome Shadow Marks her as his own.

CAN LOVE BE BORN FROM HATRED?

Shadow never intended to go through with the mating ceremony—especially with the daughter of a man he killed. But his Fever has other plans. The more he's around her, the more he craves her touch, longs to hear her voice, and aches to claim her.

From the moment Shadow's Mark formed on her hand, Breanna knew her mate-bond was destined for failure. The bounty hunter responsible for her father's death is the last wolf on this earth she could ever bind herself to forever. But if she wants to remain Alpha and save her pack, she might not have a choice. As Strider closes in on her, she finds herself relying on Shadow's quiet strength— and craving those rough hands all over her curves.

Cover designed by Kitten of Deranged Doctor Design
Interior design and formatting by Champagne Formats
Copy editing by Susie of Red Adept Editing
Proofreading by Kristina of Red Adept Editing
Indigo Dreamer Press logo designed by Indi99o of 99designs
Author photograph by Sara Rogers Photography

www.lolataylorbooks.com
www.indigodreamerpress.com

INDIGO
DREAMER PRESS

ISBN-10: 0-9835131-7-1
ISBN-13: 978-0-9835131-7-9

CHAPTER ONE

SHADOW'S NOSE SHRIVELED UP THE SECOND HE SMELLED the graveyard.

Holy shit.

This made roadkill smell good. It was a mixture of three very distinct smells: rotting flesh, decaying vegetation, with a hint of mildewed earth.

Mildewed earth that smelled like piss.

Jacque, his cocky-ass French informant, had been right about this being the hideout of those lowlife vampires. Vampires who decided it would be fun to go on a killing spree, make national news, and leave the bones of their victims on people's doorsteps. You know, for shits and giggles.

Only, when it was the bones of children you were talking about, people didn't much find that funny. The killers hadn't discriminated between paranormal or human victims, either. They'd killed everything from witchlings to werewolf pups to human children, all abducted from malls, playgrounds, and other public venues across the nation. Though the human race and paranormals had their differences and were a long way off from coexisting peacefully, both sides could agree on the fact that those serial killers were the real monsters.

Shadow grinned, knowing his eyes were glowing gold with the promise of shredding those psychotic child-killing motherfuckers to pieces.

Oh, he was going to enjoy this.

And from the bloodthirsty smiles on his comrades' faces, they were thinking the exact same thing.

They crept through the thick undergrowth of the forest surrounding the old graveyard, the tangle of brambles cutting any exposed pieces of skin. Namely, their pretty faces.

None of them gave a shit, though. Shadow knew they didn't. Not even Naomi, who might as well be Barbie when she wasn't on duty. Their skin was mostly scars, as if someone had decided to take a knife and play Picasso on their asses.

The rest of their very ripped, and very deadly, bodies were covered in sleek, black military-grade synthetic suits that fit like second skins. A howling black wolf head emblem was stamped on their right sleeves, just below their shoulders. The sigil was damn near invisible, if not for its glossy surface shining against the matte finish of the suit. The emblem was visible outright only to those who knew where to look for it, or for the matching tattoos they all wore on their bodies. The rite of passage to earning that tattoo, to taking the Blood Oath of the Black Moon Pack, was legendary.

Shadow hadn't come across a single Black Moon bounty hunter outside of his crew. Sometimes, he thought the "top-secret international organization" he worked for was more like a private club.

Some quit.

Of those who were left, few survived. And those who did… well, let's just say they'd earned Shadow's irrefutable respect.

His crew, made up of five men and two women, halted and knelt at the edge of the forest, blending in with the shadows as easily as if they were made of them.

"Are you in position?" came a man's voice from the earpiece in the captain's ear. Shadow glanced at his commander, who knelt next to him, and adjusted his weight as his bad foot started to fall asleep. The subtle shift in movement resulted in him brushing shoulders with the man who led them, the same man who'd saved his life and became his best friend for the past six years he'd been in service.

The brief contact was comforting, familiar.

A reminder he wasn't alone anymore.

Still fucking weird, but after a lifetime of solitude, he wasn't complaining.

"Fucking A," Captain Riley murmured back, his voice barely audible above the rustling of leaves and other foresty shit that sashayed and swayed around them in the autumn breeze.

Shadow's nose tingled as the wind kicked up dirt and

pollen off the forest floor. Hey, at least it was carrying that godforsaken stench downwind. For the first time in a mile, he felt as if he could take a full breath.

From his left, Naomi stifled a gasp. "Holy hell, that was rank," she muttered.

"Keep your voice down," Riley snapped.

Shadow caught something that sounded like, "Don't get your panties in a bunch, princess," but it was difficult to tell over the symphony of chirping crickets, belching frogs, and dancing leaves.

Riley let the quip roll off of him without so much as a snarl.

There was an unspoken rule that Riley's orders were indisputable, even if you didn't entirely agree with them. Sure, they may joke around, but when it came down to it they knew who was in charge.

And if they ever needed a reminder… well, all they had to do was glance at the twisted flesh morphing Riley's face, arms, pretty much every damn inch of his body, to remember what that son of a bitch was capable of.

In broad daylight, it was hard not to stare at Riley's ugly mug. Cloaked in the shadows of night, he became downright mesmerizing, like a demon straight out of your worst nightmare. You wanted to look away, if only out of politeness or the fact that looking at him made you want to piss your pants, but you just *couldn't*.

Darkness pooled in the trenches of razed flesh that had been dug by wicked claws nearly twenty years ago. Riley shouldn't have been alive after falling into a cave of demons, but if anyone could make miracles happen, it was him. He'd been tracking them for days as part of his latest mission. Heaven and hell had strict rules about full-blooded angels and demons being on this plane of existence, and let's just say the demons had broken all the rules and then some. Riley had known he was close to finding them and had gotten reckless. No one saw the hidden entrance to the cave where the demons were hiding out until Riley fell through the earth and plunged straight into a horror movie.

He should have been dead. Really, he should have. Any other wolf or paranormal would have been killed in a heartbeat, but not Riley.

Shadow had once seen the man decapitate three vampires using a butter knife. His boss took ingenuity to a whole other level. If not for his creative use of a vial of holy water and a simple wooden stake, the demons would have done a whole lot worse than marked up his body with their claws and teeth.

The whole "demon slayer" thing was a legend among their troop by now. He'd thought Thompson, their newest recruit, was going to shit a brick when Shadow had first told him the tale.

"Making the im-fucking-possible possible." That was Riley's slogan.

And thank God for it. Otherwise, Shadow might not be breathing this rank-ass air right now.

"On my mark, move in," said the gruff voice through the earpiece. Riley's boss, whom they all affectionately called "Midnight." No one knew what he looked like, except for Riley, and they sure as hell weren't getting any answers out of that poker-faced douche bag. They'd all speculated, of course. Judging by his voice, Midnight was in his midfifties, with graying hair shaved in a military cut, cool, steely eyes, and a mouth that was perpetually stuck in a frown.

Riley didn't much like them talking about Midnight. Shadow had once tried prying the reason why out of him, but in typical Riley fashion, he'd changed the subject.

"And no matter what you think when you see them, remember what they've done," added Midnight sternly. "These vamps are evil. They are the enemy, plain and simple."

"It's black and white," Riley said, keen eyes fixed upon the silent graveyard. "No problem. For a quarter of a million dollars apiece for this bounty, we won't second-guess."

A promise, or a command, whichever way you looked at it. And just what the hell did Midnight mean by "no matter what you think when you see them?" Did the vamps look weird? They were *child-killers*. It didn't matter what the hell they looked like. Shadow was going to enjoy the shit out of putting a couple of bullets through their heads. Or maybe Shifting into his wolf form and taking his time with killing them in a more creative, satisfying way. None of his teammates was above torture, especially when the one suffering deserved it and then some.

A moment of silence passed, filled with the sounds of the night. Shadow scanned the graveyard. Even the dead bodies of paranormal creatures gave off signatures, which those vampire bastards were probably using to mask their own.

No matter. If he couldn't sense their paranormal signatures and hone in on their exact location, then his nose sure as hell could sniff them out.

Just follow the scent of stale piss and body odor. If it smells like a Dumpster at noon in July, it must be a vampire.

Shadow felt Riley tense before he heard the command.

"Go," Midnight clipped.

Riley raised a hand and pointed. As one they moved out, guns ready, footsteps silent. A lethal, synchronized unit. They knew each other's movements. Knew one another's fighting styles. Riley had taken special care with his team. Even after they'd lost one of their own last year on a mission gone bad, Riley had put the candidates through hell and back before at last selecting Thompson. The kid might be a bit green, but he was second only to Riley when it came to fucking shit up. Seriously, even Shadow, sadistic as he could be in the heat of battle, got the heebie-jeebies sometimes when watching Thompson do his thing.

It took less than thirty seconds to surround the graveyard and get into position. One wolf every ten feet, spread out equally around the circumference of the graveyard.

A light fog had moved in, covering the ground and all but the tops of the crooked tombstones. A darkened mausoleum stood at the graveyard's center. Not even a fence wrapped around the place. It was old as dirt, with some of the graves dating back to the Revolutionary War. The earth had sunken in at spots, tipping a few gravestones into one another, while the rest lay chipped or broken in the dirt. Most were so weatherworn you couldn't even read the writing on them anymore.

Shadow idly wondered if when he died he'd even get a gravestone, and if he did, if they'd put his real name on it. Either way, he didn't think he much cared. Being forgotten might not be so bad, considering all the wicked things he'd done since joining the Black Moon Pack.

Better to let the world think he'd never existed.

The wind shifted, carrying the smell of decaying bodies toward Shadow's direction. Bracing himself, he took shallower breaths. Inside his head, Thompson sputtered and cursed through the telepathic link all members of a pack shared.

Good God! It's choking me! Thompson said.

Must be fresh kills, sometime within the past two weeks, murmured Orion, a tall tank of a man with dark skin, hazel eyes ringed in gold, and thick ropes of dreadlocks he always kept pulled halfway back. Orion was from New Orleans and more than a little versed in voodoo, so Shadow had wanted the Southerner's code name to be "Spooky," but Orion would have none of it.

All the more reason to get this taken care of, fast, Riley said. *Shadow, you're up.*

On it. Shadow slinked into the graveyard, bending and twisting his body so as to remain hidden in the darkest shadows. There was a reason he was named after them. Growing up in the slums of New York City, he'd quickly learned that the difference between jail time and remaining free lay in your ability to hide and keep moving while staying out of sight. When your momma was MIA and your dad too drunk to care about cooking dinner or paying the bills, you had to get real clever real fast about finding food and money. So from the time he was seven to the time he turned eighteen and left that shit hole for good, he'd had plenty of practice at "turning into a shadow."

Luckily for him, the graveyard had plenty of them. The thick cloud cover overhead helped in that department, obscuring the full, bloodred moon just enough to hide his swift progress through the graveyard.

Though he'd rather dump a tub of oil over himself and light a match, he forced the putrid air in and out of his nostrils, sifting through the smells of death and latching on to the vampires' perfume of stale piss. He still hadn't felt signatures yet. No surprise. A lot of vamps had magic, and it wasn't the first time he'd come across someone who could hide their paranormal signatures. Though a valiant effort, it hadn't saved them, just as it sure as hell wouldn't save these sons of bitches.

As he crouched behind a large tombstone covered in black ivy, he bit back a curse as the phantom injury flared up in his foot. He'd earned it while stealing goods from a supermarket owned by a local crime lord—a move he would not recommend, but hey, he was desperate, young, and stupid at the time. The security guard was kind enough to leave him a reminder not to be so stupid by giving him a bullet in his foot as he'd been running away. The medical bills for removing the bullet and patching up his foot were steep, considering he had no insurance. He'd evaded paying them by moving from city to city, often twice within the same month. He thought his foot would be permanently fucked up until he fell in with the Black Moon Pack, finally got some decent fucking money, settled his many debts, and was able to visit a doctor who knew what the fuck she was doing. "Surgery will help it," his shiny new doctor had said. And by help, she'd obviously meant fuck it up beyond repair, because that was exactly what she'd done. Not even a Blue Witch or Warlock could heal that kind of fuck-uppery. He'd sued the shit out of the doctor, of course, and while more money was always nice, it couldn't buy back the full use of his foot. It made him a liability.

One he was seriously afraid Riley would cull someday very soon, for the safety of the team.

Fuck, Shadow didn't know what the hell he'd do without the Black Moon Pack. Roam? Get a nine-to-five day job, like civilized folk? God, that sounded like dying and going to hell right there. He'd rather gouge his eyes out than work a desk job.

He could picture his resume now. *"So, Mr., um, Shadow. We see you have a background in 'fucking people up' and 'killing a lot of shit,' and yet you have no record. Care to explain?"*

Knowing his temper, some paper-pushing manager would try to get cute with him. And he'd get real cute right back by bashing his face into his desk.

Yeah, he'd have to rethink the desk-job idea.

Shadow's bad foot screamed in pain, making him wince.

That foot bothering you again? Riley asked quietly. Shadow knew the question would be directed only at him through a private link. Riley was a lot of things, but at least the guy was courteous.

Shadow shrugged off the question. The silent "Can you do your job?" *Eh, it's the weather.*

My busted knee does the same thing. Don't sweat it, man. Translation—I don't let my injuries interfere with my job because I'm a badass motherfucker, and you'd better not let yours interfere either. *Picked up on anything yet?*

Shadow gave the graveyard one last scan for good measure. *Nope. Just me, the pack, a whole lotta dead, rotting things stuffed somewhere around here—in the mausoleum, I'm guessing—and a whole lotta gravestones and—*

Child-like laughter filled the graveyard, the sweet, delicate sounds echoing off the tombstones. Shadows ran through the mist, faster than even his wolf eyes could catch a glimpse of.

The electric tingle of paranormal signatures had the hairs all along his body standing upright in unison. *There's three of them, from what I can tell,* Shadow said through their pack-bond. He didn't bother saying they were all vamps. If he'd felt it, the others had too. And judging from the tension crackling through their bond, they certainly had.

Swish!

Something whizzed by, and sharp pain lit up Shadow's cheek. Son of a—

The tang of blood filled the air as warm liquid dribbled down his face. That motherfucker had cut him.

"You taste sweeter than you look."

With a shriek at the innocent, young voice, he whirled, gun raised and pointed at…

At—a *child*?

At first, he thought maybe the vampire's claws had been dipped in poison, which had seeped into his bloodstream and begun to fuck with his perception of reality.

Because this kid, this innocent little person no older than five, couldn't have glowing red eyes. Or little, cherubic hands stained in dried blood.

Or tiny fangs poking just beneath her upper lip.

The little girl—the *vampire*—sucked on her fingers as she watched him like a hawk eyeing a mouse. "That's the first time I've had full-grown wolf blood. It's different from what I expected. Sweeter. Judas told me not to drink it because it's poisonous, but Mr. Tavers says that's just an urban myth."

He didn't know who the hell she was talking about, but listening to her talk threw his mind for a loop. For one, the kid still had a child-like tone of voice, very high-pitched and sweet, but she spoke with the grace of a thirty-year-old woman.

Secondly, his face had been clawed by *that*? No one snuck up on him. Ever. And the first person to do so was a fucking toddler.

Lowering his gun a fraction, but not enough so as to be stupid, he said gently, "How old are you?"

She smiled. "It's impolite to ask a lady her age."

The fuck? Was she *flirting* with him? Nausea kicked his stomach, and he nearly hurled right there. "Are you, um, lost?"

"No. This is my home."

"The graveyard?"

"The dead don't seem to mind." A careless shrug,

though those crimson eyes still stared at his face. It had begun to itch—the cuts were scabbing over. Thank God for accelerated healing, courtesy of his werewolf genes. "I want some more," she said, licking the blood off her lips. She took a step forward, her feet bare and covered in so much dirt and blood that it looked as if she were wearing brown socks.

He threw up a hand. "Not so fast, sister. You have some explaining to do."

She stopped, eyes going wide and bottom lip trembling. "Am I in trouble?"

He studied her. "I don't think so. But your master might be."

"Master?"

"Your maker. Someone had to have turned you."

A snarl tore out of her throat, and she hissed, baring her fangs. "You think I answer to a master? I haven't needed a master in four hundred years."

Say what? "I'm sorry, I thought you said 'four hundred years.'"

"I did." She smiled sweetly. Any trace of her animalistic rage vanished in a few blinks of her doe-like eyes.

He didn't like where this was going. "And your master released you, I assume."

"He didn't have a choice—I killed him. Ripped his throat out with these." She tapped her delicate little fangs.

Fuck. She hadn't blinked twice when saying that she'd killed her master, either. His breathing quickened, and he threw open his senses.

A twig snapped to his right; someone was moving in.

And judging from the rotting smell and the tingling vampire signature, it wasn't one of his buddies to back him up. A third paranormal signature crackled along his skin, to his left, this one stronger than the others.

Shit.

He was about to be ambushed.

Keep her distracted, Riley ordered. *We're moving in.*

Hurry the fuck up before she and her buddies decide to have a midnight werewolf snack.

"Who are you talking to?"

His eyes snapped back to the little girl's. "Excuse me?"

"Inside your head just now. Do you have company?" She peered about.

His jaw dropped.

Telepathic. This freaking toddler vamp was telepathic.

With an exasperated groan, he rolled his shoulders. "You have got to be kidd—"

Gunfire rang out, shattering the symphony of the night. Something shrieked and went down hard on the ground.

The little girl whirled, hissing. Then she was gone in a blink, her platinum-blond hair streaking behind her and making her look like a ghost playing amongst the graves.

Chills crept up Shadow's arms, making his skin tingle.

To your right! cried out Naomi's voice.

A shadow loomed in the corner of his eye. Cursing and twisting on the balls of his feet, he raised the gun and fired—into thin air. A few seconds later, claws gripped his shoulders and violently yanked him back. The rear of his skull crashed into a tombstone, making him see stars.

Something knelt in front of him, sniffing. "You wolves really are too arrogant for your own good," came a cultured voice filled with disdain. "You honestly thought you could sneak up on a master vampire?"

The man squatting in front of him was in his late thirties, with golden hair cropped above his shoulders, an open white button-down shirt—also sporting the blood-stained look so many vamps found fashionable—and trousers that looked as if they were from a few centuries ago. He too wore no shoes. Flickering crimson light sparkled in his eyes.

Shadow bared his fangs. The reflection from his glowing golden eyes shone in the vamp's. "She said she had no master. That she killed him."

"And she did—kill me, that is." He smiled, showing off two large fangs. "Then she turned me into her servant for all eternity. Ironic, huh? That's Lady Luck for you. She'll kiss you one second then kick you in the balls the next, just for fun."

Someone screamed—Thompson? Orion?—followed by more gunfire. The sounds of struggle and the scent of fresh blood filled the air.

Sensing his team's distress, Shadow started to get up, when Big Bad Vampire pushed him back down. He dug his claws into Shadow's shoulder, pinning him to the gravestone. "Vicious little thing, my Anne." An amused chuckle. "I'll never be able to match her talent for raw savagery."

"Why the hell did you kill all those kids? For sport? Out of boredom?"

He cocked his head to the side, confused. "I didn't

have anything to do with it." He leaned forward, his demonic eyes locked with Shadow's. "That was all Anne's idea."

The child? All those murders... Toddler Vamp did that?

"Give me a break," Shadow spat. "You're probably trying to cover your own tracks by throwing her under the bus."

"It's true, actually."

The girl appeared behind the older vampire and rested her hand on his shoulder. He flinched. Shadow's eyes narrowed. Was he... was he actually *afraid* of her?

"I've never liked children," she went on matter-of-factly.

"But you are one."

"No, I am not!" she roared, coming within an inch of Shadow's face and hissing. Blood and gore dripped from her mouth. The smell... *Oh God. Naomi!*

He started to struggle again, but the man's claws dug in that much deeper, tearing flesh. "Don't move while the lady is talking to you!"

"I have hated every child I've ever come across," Anne hissed. "Liars, monsters, all of them. They said they liked me, that they wanted to be my friends. But then they hurt me. They teased and bullied me as a human for my mind-reading abilities. Called me a freak and threatened to burn me at the stake, or stone me to death, all for simply being different. I didn't ask for this gift. I didn't ask to be treated like dirt. I finally said no more. Children are the most villainous tormentors on earth. Childhood is cruel, one long test to see if you've got what it takes to survive to

16

adulthood."

He could only stare. This was the kid's outlook on her peers? What the hell had her life been like?

"You want to know what my life was like?" Anne said.

That was right. In his bewilderment, he'd forgotten he was dealing with a telepath.

"My parents left me on the steps of an orphanage. Mr. Tavers"—she jerked a thumb at the man—"was our overseer. I say overseer because that place was like a slave camp. We were made to do all the chores and to answer at his beck and call. He even made us work all day and well into the night at his laundry business. The rooms where we worked were either so cold we could see our breaths, or they were so hot some of us died of heat stroke. Many of us died of exhaustion, starvation, or disease. We never got presents, never got birthday cakes. No kisses, no hugs, no signs of affection."

"And I'll bet that made you angry."

Her silent glare was answer enough. Couldn't say he blamed her. Not that his childhood was Hallmark-movie worthy, but hell, it had been heaven compared to what this little girl had been through.

"Is that why you killed all those children?" Shadow asked quietly.

Anne blinked. "They deserved it."

"Did they bully you, like those kids at the orphanage did four hundred years ago?"

Doubt and regret flickered through her eyes, which flashed a pretty blue hue before turning red once more. "It doesn't matter! They're guilty! I saw all of them bully someone or something—animals, playmates, siblings. They were cruel hearted, each and every one of them. They deserved what was coming to them." With a "humph," she spun about, dismissing him.

Fuck. So their child-killer had turned out to be a child herself. Midnight's warning suddenly made sense.

No matter what you think when you see them, remember what they've done.

"Remember what she's done," he murmured aloud, barely audible.

What she'd done... in her mind, he bet she thought she was doing the world a service. Saving another kid from a self-esteem beating as she had endured.

His heart suddenly went out to her. He'd never had kids, hadn't even considered it. No one in their line of work would, not if they were still sane, anyway. There didn't need to be another kid growing up in the world with a daddy or mommy who couldn't be there for them. And he refused to let some fucking stranger raise his pups. He wouldn't do that to his children, make 'em think they were unwanted.

But while slumming it, he'd been the victim of plenty of abuse at the hands of street gangs and asshats who thought they owned everything and everyone they saw. As though because their life was hard, the world owed them something. You get abused long enough, and you start to feel pretty resentful—and mad as hell. Something he could relate to firsthand. He'd spent a lot of years dealing with the aftermath of that anger, until he'd found martial arts as an outlet, a way to channel all that pent-up aggression and purge it from his body before it could do him serious harm.

This kid had most likely been holding in her pain for so long—literally, hundreds of years—that it had eventually exploded. The result? A mass murdering spree to exact her revenge on people who mirrored her childhood demons.

Immense sympathy swelled in his chest, making it hard to look at her with the knowledge that he had to end her. "I'm so sorry," he whispered.

She stopped and turned back around. "What did you say?"

His eyes lifted to hers. *Her cheeks might be round, her voice might be sweet, but she is not a child. She's a murderer, the target. Pure and simple.*

"Keep it simple," he muttered. Still, his heart picked up speed, pumping doubt into his veins.

When you were in the Black Moon Pack, you couldn't afford self-doubt. It could shut you down, which could make things very tricky indeed. And possibly result in getting you, or your pack, killed. He'd already failed Naomi and who knew how many others on his crew by not acting immediately when he saw Anne and realized what she was. He wasn't going to let the rest of them down.

He Shifted before he could overthink it and change his mind. Mr. Tavers screamed, throwing up his hands as a massive wolf, black as pitch, descended on him. Shadow pinned him with his paws and swiftly relieved him of his throat. Blech. He hated the taste of vampire blood, especially that of a vamp who'd been gorging himself on children. The thought of it made him almost throw up.

Anne ran. Shadow went after her, sensing her fear. The smells around him were amplified in his wolf form.

Three of his comrades were injured or dead, he couldn't tell. So much blood saturated the air, mingling with the stench of the corpses the trio of vamps had stashed somewhere. That was the other thing—where the hell was the third vampire? He'd felt its presence earlier via its signature, but then it had vanished.

Riley was shouting something at him telepathically, but the chase was on. His prey drive overshadowed his common sense. Shadow tore after Anne, leaping over gravestones as though they were nothing.

Anne burst through the mausoleum doors and skidded to a halt in front of the far wall. She whirled about, eyes wide with fear.

Gotcha.

Shadow leapt.

As his jaws opened wide, prepared to sever her head, his humanity screamed at him to stop.

She's just a child, a victim!

And above all other oaths the pack had sworn, they said they'd never harm an innocent.

Yes, she'd killed.

Yes, she was a liability.

But he saw only a little girl thrown into a monster's body, harboring years of hatred for the cruel hand life had dealt her. It wasn't fair—she didn't deserve to die. She needed a second chance. And the longer he looked at her, the more he saw his little sister, Amelia, in her eyes. A hurting soul, crying out for help the only way she knew how.

Through violence and death, just as the world had showed her.

Amelia hadn't gotten a second chance, and for that, Shadow had failed her. Failed to protect her. Failed to keep his promise to his mother before she'd skipped town when he was a kid.

But for Anne, life didn't have to be so cruel.

The biting urge to save her gnawed at him until he couldn't take it anymore.

Veering to the right, he snarled and slammed into a row of coffins lining one side of the mausoleum. The old structure shuddered, raining dust and debris down from the ceiling. His paws scraped against the stone floors as he righted himself, panting hard as he eyed the vampire staring at him with mouth agape.

"You stopped," she said. "You really shouldn't have."

Nails scraped along the insides of the coffins. Shadow growled, whirling about as lids opened and fell to the floor. Tiny white hands reached out, hefting up little bodies that were asleep before now.

Before their master awakened them.

Pair after pair of red eyes lit up the inside of the mausoleum, until the crimson light drowned out the moonlight drifting through a lonely hole in the ceiling.

The ground began to tremble beneath his paws. With dread, he chanced a glance at the graveyard. The earth stirred, looking like a roiling sea that tipped over the gravestones. Like something straight out of a zombie flick, tiny hands shot out of the earth. Bodies emerged from the soil, rank skin dripping off of shattered bones. Some were missing limbs or an eye, an ear, or in the case of one particularly gruesome corpse, a head. From the size of their bodies, they were all children, just like those that stared at him in the mausoleum. Only, unlike his glowing red-eyed friends, the corpses out in the graveyard weren't vampires.

They were the walking dead. The stench that had filled the air, all the bodies of the missing children that had never been recovered… Anne had been stowing them away in the graveyard for safekeeping.

To use as a trap. And if the dead could walk, that meant she had a—

Boots clicked on the stone floor of the mausoleum as a figure stepped out of the shadows. A handsome young man in his teens stepped into the pool of red-stained moonlight, palms raised toward the ceiling. Pools of murky green light gathered in his hands, shimmering with faint red sparks.

The vampire stopped beside Anne, red eyes fixed on Shadow and a wicked grin on his fanged face.

"Your friends were fun but no match for my power," the boy said. He had dark-blond hair styled in a tousled look and pale skin that matched Anne's. His clothing was also not from this century, more like circa 1700s.

"Judas was also shunned by society in his time," Anne said, admiring her child. She stroked his arm lovingly, like petting a favorite animal. "Like me, he was an outcast for his abilities. Whereas I could read minds, Judas could bring back and control the dead. As I'm sure a wolf of your expertise knows, necromancy is an extremely rare gift. I couldn't let it go to waste. So when he sought me out and begged me to turn him, I did. He understands me. He's the only person who knows what it's like to be me."

More screaming came behind him as the dead crawled free of their graves. Though gunfire still rang out, there wasn't as much of it.

His pack was losing.

Ivy—the only other female on the team besides Naomi—cursed. Her wail pierced the air, and a moment later the dead began moaning and hissing. The sounds of tearing flesh rang in Shadow's ears—a feeding frenzy.

Oh God. Ivy! he screamed.

Shadow, fucking listen to me! I've been screaming at you for five minutes! Get out of there! Riley yelled back. *Abort the mission! I repeat, abort—*

Stark silence. Their telepathic pack channel was completely void of life. He felt his pack's absence down to his core. It was as if his own soul had been ripped out, leaving him feeling empty and very alone. He tipped back his head and let loose a pained howl.

Shadow's heart pounded. How the fuck had Midnight missed the enormous power these vampires had? These were far from normal vamps they were dealing with. Why the hell hadn't he said anything?

Unless… unless he'd meant to leave it out because he'd wanted the team to fail.

But to what end? It didn't make sense.

Shadow's mind spun with questions and theories, none of them pleasant.

"I guess you'll never get to find out. Soon, it won't matter anyway." Anne looked at Judas and nodded. "Kill him."

Shit. He had to get the fuck out of there, had to—

His body slammed to the floor as the child vampires waiting in the coffins leapt onto his back, pinning him.

His skin lit up with red-hot pain as fangs sank into his flesh, tearing and sucking. The venom from one bite wouldn't kill him; that much he knew. But from fifty or so vamps…

He fought to buck them off, but where he freed himself of one, another latched on like a leech. They dug their claws into his fur to anchor themselves to him.

As the venom spread through his system, slowed his mind, and blurred his vision, he kept thinking of his teammates.

Of all the good and bad times they'd had together, like a big, dysfunctional family.

What have I done?

His vision started to turn black, zapping his strength to live along with it. His body felt so heavy, as if he were slowly turning to stone. He fell to the floor, his head slumped toward the entrance.

Clouds had moved in, obscuring the moon. Then the cloud cover shifted, raining red moonlight down on the grisly scene below.

The graveyard was soaked in blood. Pieces of his teammates littered the ground. A shred of torn, dark flesh bearing the wolf head tattoo lay by the mausoleum—it had come from Orion.

There was no more gunfire.

No more screams.

As the vampires continued to feed off him, and the darkness overcame all conscious thought, there was at last no remembrance of the guilt he felt at having failed his entire team because he'd hesitated to kill his target.

Because he'd been too soft.

Too weak.

Not enough. He was never enough.

Not strong enough to save his team. Not strong enough to save Amelia.

Not even strong enough to save himself.

CHAPTER TWO

Three years later

SHADOW KNEW THEY WERE BEING FOLLOWED BEFORE they stepped off the plane. Call him paranoid, but after being snuck up on too many times to count, he'd learned to watch his back every damn second.

And, more recently, he'd learned to watch his Alpha's back.

Drake Jones looked more like royalty than the leader of some rough-and-tumble werewolf pack. With a wardrobe that consisted of fancy suits, polished dress shoes, and watches worth more than Shadow's salary, the middle-aged Alpha was rocking the style thing.

He flashed a smile at the flight attendant as they exited the plane. Though the man could definitely afford a private jet, Drake always liked flying coach. He "liked to mingle," something Shadow never had been very good at. Which was fine by him. Mingling wasn't in his job description;

busting skulls to keep his Alpha safe was.

The rest of Drake's security team, headed by Shadow, fanned out to their positions as their Alpha made his way through the terminal. People stopped and stared as he passed, probably wondering if he was somebody famous.

Shadow broke off from the group. *I have something to attend to,* he telepathically told his second-in-command, Bronx.

The thickly muscled, dark-skinned man caught his eye and silently nodded. With his black suit and dress shirt, he looked more like a member of the mob than a bodyguard. They all did. The wardrobe was Drake's idea. The thought was that the more intimidating they looked, the better they'd scare people off. You know, in case anyone got the bright idea in their head to actually attempt an attack on Drake.

If only it worked that way. If only it were that easy to stop an attack before it happened.

Shadow turned into a bathroom marked Closed For Repairs. The inside was silent. The floor and most of the stalls were torn up, as if it was in the middle of a remodel. The air smelled like dust.

Shadow waited in the center of the room. A moment later the door opened.

He smirked. "Was wondering when you'd make a move."

He whirled and punched so quickly the man didn't have time to block. The air rushed out of him as he stumbled backward. Shadow lunged, following up with an open palm strike to the guy's chin. He went flying into the wall, crashing into a pile of wood.

The knife he'd been clutching fell to the ground.

Shadow stalked forward as the guy groaned and made to retrieve the knife. Shadow knelt in front of him, scooped up the knife, and dangled it in front of the stranger's stunned face. "And what were you planning on doing with this?"

The man had a hard time focusing on the knife. Considering how hard Shadow had hit him, he was probably seeing double. "I was… going… to kill you…"

"Why?" Shadow asked pleasantly.

The man's voice smoldered with anger. "Because you killed my son, you asshole. Don't try denying it. I know it was you."

"What was your son's name?" he asked, not without compassion.

His bottom lip trembled as emotion swam in his eyes. "Mark."

A nod. "And was Mark involved in any illegal activities?"

Silence.

That was what he thought. He raised a brow.

"He…" A hard swallow. "He used to bleed vampires and sell their blood on the Black Market."

"A Red Rum dealer, then. Or, if he wasn't into creating and selling liquor that can kill you, perhaps he dealt in Stardust?"

"Stardust?"

"A vampire's blood can be magically processed to form this pink powder called Stardust. It looks innocent, but it's anything but. It makes the druggie hallucinate. I once watched a man gouge out his own eyes after snorting the stuff, convinced worms were crawling out of him."

"Jesus!"

"Look," Shadow said with a hard sigh, "I'm not in that line of work anymore, killing people for money, that is. And I'm sorry about your son."

The man voiced his disbelief in a few choice words.

Shadow ignored him. He was used to jabs at his questionable moral compass. "But I can tell you my former employer never had us go after innocents or casual drug dealers. Your son must have done something a lot worse to deserve his fate."

"Go to hell!" The man spit in his face. Tears ran down his cheeks as he silently fumed at Shadow, probably wishing to set him on fire with his glare.

So he didn't know the truth about his son. Soon as he said the name, Shadow knew whom he was talking about. Mark's dad had a tattoo on his left hand of a feather. So had Mark. That was how he'd put two and two together. Mark hadn't simply dealt in illegal drugs—he'd also been involved in the kidnapping and trafficking of young human girls. He'd started his own underground company, specializing in products made from vampire blood. And he'd needed sustenance for the vampires he'd kept chained in the basement of his secret warehouse…

Shadow pocketed the knife, a simple switchblade, and left the man sobbing alone in the bathroom. He most likely would never see him again. Or maybe he would. The ones who held deep grudges bordering on rage were like a dog with a bone. They didn't give up the chase that easily.

Except his life was the bone, and he had no intention of handing it over anytime soon.

Drake was waiting for him in the limo parked out front.

Shadow got in without a word, and the driver took off. The two men rode in silence before Drake finally spoke. "So," he said casually, "who was trying to kill you this time?"

Drake had sought out Shadow with the intention of employing him after firing his previous head of security for incompetence. The ex–chief of security had seemed keener on watching porn on his phone than protecting his boss. Once Drake had done the research on Shadow's background, he'd become persistent in making him the top of his security team. "A man with your skills is hard to come by," he'd said. "And the world isn't getting any nicer."

He should have been dead after getting bitten that many times by vampires. And after passing out and waking up in an Underworld hospital a week later, thanks to Midnight's backup team saving his ass, Shadow had wished he had died. He had failed his pack—miserably.

After losing his entire team in the vampire disaster, he had promptly quit Black Moon, Inc. and vanished. At first he'd traveled. Then when he'd gotten bored with that, he'd moved from town to town, working odd jobs. He never was one to be content staying in one place for long. Or, at least, that was what he'd kept telling himself.

Really, he was just trying to outrun the pain of his past. But that's the thing about guilt—it follows you everywhere.

Eventually, the itch to return to what he did best—protect the interests of humanity and the Underworld—returned. That was when Drake swooped into his life. They'd been introduced through a mutual friend at a soiree. Then Drake had started digging into Shadow's past, liked what he'd found, and made an offer Shadow couldn't refuse. By then Shadow had blown through his savings and was on the verge of declaring bankruptcy.

What was left of his moral compass had tried dissuading Drake from hiring him. Shadow had enemies, a plethora of them. Enemies who could just as easily hurt Drake as they could him. He'd be a liability. Drake was convinced otherwise. When Shadow had at last gotten evicted for not paying rent again and had to spend the night in a homeless shelter, he'd finally taken up Drake on his offer.

Drake was still staring at him, waiting for an answer.

"No one," Shadow replied, looking out the window.

Drake chuckled. "You don't have to be ashamed of who you were. I admire the kind of bravery it took to do what you did. You saved a lot of lives."

"And destroyed twice as many." Shadow's gaze became hard. "A lot of families will never get their kids, spouses, or siblings back because of what I did."

Drake watched him with sad eyes. "At some point, you need to stop blaming yourself. You had a mission, and you fulfilled it. I can't think of anything more honorable than trying to protect your fellow Americans."

Shadow looked away again, this time positioning his body toward the window. Conversation closed. He fucking hated it when people pretended he was some kind of goddamned hero. People saw what they wanted to see, even if the villain was sitting right in front of them.

The drive to Castle Crescent, the site of the werewolf royalty gathering, wasn't far. Settled in the rolling countryside of Arkansas, the Scottish castle looked out of place. The werewolf king, Victor Crescent, had it brought over stone by stone and reconstructed. A large garden lay spread out behind the castle, and cars were lined up along the circular driveway that looped in front of the castle's entrance.

The driver stopped. A footman opened the door, and Shadow got out first. With a glance around, he nodded, and Drake joined him.

"Try not to look so excited," Drake said, nudging him as they walked up the gazillion flights of stone steps leading to the open doors of the castle. The rest of Drake's security team flanked him on either side, eyes darting this way and that, searching for threats.

Shadow smiled. He'd trained them well.

While he admired his team, they weren't family. He could never seem to accomplish the closeness he had with the Black Moon Pack. Probably because he kept turning down social invitations. He couldn't get too close, not again. When he got close to people, they got hurt. He wouldn't be responsible for another pack's demise when the weight of his comrades' deaths still hung around his shoulders like a leaden cape.

Shadow grunted in response to Drake's teasing. He fucking hated these events. He'd rather scrub toilets than fancy up with a bunch of snotty royals.

Cold eyes surveyed him and his team quickly as they entered the castle. Many looked away, no doubt dismissing him as more "hired help." Some stared.

And some glared at him so hotly he thought his flesh would start to melt.

Yeah, he was used to being hated. Didn't mean he liked it.

Many of the royals in this room had business deals go south because he'd offed one of the people involved in the deals. Tons of money had been lost as a result, which had earned him the title of "Resident Asshole." Never mind how hypocritical that was, considering most of these bratty asshats were corrupt as all get-out.

Did he mention he hated royals?

A woman wearing a scrap of cloth for a dress that probably cost thousands of dollars sashayed by him, winking. His inner wolf surged to the surface, whining to rut. He firmly pushed it back down.

Dammit, now was not the time for his Fever to kick into high gear. Every werewolf knew when their Blood Moon was upon them. The urge to mate was insatiable. Only, he hadn't Marked anyone yet. Probably because he refused to bed anyone. All part of his "do not let anyone get close" policy.

It was just as well if he never found a mate. If his Blood Moon passed without him mating, he would be "doomed" never to fall in love again. Which suited him fine. The fewer people who were intimately involved with him, the better.

Drake clapped him on the back, oblivious that the

head of his security was in the throes of his Fever. Shadow hadn't told him. Hadn't seen the need to. The Alpha had enough on his plate as it was.

"I promise I'll only schmooze for a little bit. Then we'll raid the liquor bar." Drake grinned. His teeth were so white they could probably glow in the dark. "What do you say?"

Did someone mention liquor?

"Sure," Shadow said gruffly then followed his Alpha, literally, into the wolves' den.

CHAPTER THREE

STRIDER WAS ABOUT TO GET A BLACK EYE, COURTESY OF her fist. Seriously, they'd been at the summit all of an hour before the groping had begun.

Steeling herself, Breanna clenched her fists at her side. Her lips barely moved as she growled quietly, "Remove your hand from my ass at once, or I'll remove it for you. And if I have to remove it, I promise you'll need surgery to reattach it."

A low rumble of a chuckle came from behind her as a tall, finely built man strode forward. Towering six inches over her already impressive five ten, Strider was as wicked as he was tall. And not in a good way. She'd seen the way the man toyed with his prey while on joint-pack hunts. No one who enjoyed inflicting suffering that much would ever share her bed. And he sure as hell would never share her pack. She'd give her life before subjecting them to his cruel whims.

"I have to admit, your spunk turns me on," he said, flashing a devilish grin as he unabashedly looked her down and up again. "As does that strip of cloth you call a dress. I must say, my imagination has been spot-on."

Ugh. She didn't bother hiding the cringe that wrinkled up her face. Sure, the black silk dress was provocative, hanging onto her lithe form with a few straps of diamonds. The back was completely out, dipping to the top of her ass and showing off the Whiteclaw Pack tattoo inked onto the small of her back—a white paw print centered at the trough of two crisscrossed feathers.

But seriously, did Strider have to look her over as though she were a piece of meat?

"I think I threw up a little in my mouth," she said, giving him a fake smile. "Excuse me while I go find some champagne to wash out the taste."

She didn't wait for his permission to leave. Turning on her heel, she stalked away... far, far away.

Soon as she was around the corner, she leaned against the wall, closed her eyes, and sighed hard. The sounds of orchestral music and stiff, polite conversation drifted toward her ears. Breanna looked about glumly.

This castle, these people... for all their beauty, they were so tarnished. Insincere. And if there was one thing she couldn't stand, it was people who smiled to your face and stabbed you in the back the moment you turned away.

Which meant, regrettably, that she couldn't stand ninety percent of the people in the room. She needed to get out of here, needed to run and be free from sacrificing her personal desires over worry for her pack's well-being.

But she knew that was never going to happen. So long as she was Alpha, she would never stop worrying over her pack's safety.

"The pack comes first," her father said to her when she was a teenaged Alpha-in-training. "Never forget that."

Oh, she wouldn't. How could she, when her father had reminded her at every turn while she was growing up that the pack came before all else, even his own daughter?

The bitter taste of resentment washed over her tongue. She had been tempted once to flee, to fling away her responsibilities just to spite her father's wishes.

To maybe, finally, get his attention.

But that would have been selfish. There were good people in her pack, people who both needed and counted on her. She couldn't let them down, not even to save herself.

Being an Alpha royally sucked sometimes.

She felt Jack's presence before she saw him casually lean against the wall, next to her. Perpetually tanned, with thick blond hair that hung down to his shoulders, and cerulean eyes, he was easy to look at. Breanna had considered bedding him once. They were both drunk and were at a Halloween party hosted by a neighboring pack they had an alliance with. There'd been… something between them, though she never figured out what. Later, she was thankful her common sense had overturned her lust, and they hadn't gone through with anything. Her relationships with the people in her pack were complicated enough without throwing a friends-with-benefits scenario into the mix.

A duo of female wolves walked by, casting Jack

admiring glances. He happily obliged them with one of his token panty-dropping smiles. "Having fun yet?" he said as he offered her a glass of champagne. He let his eyes linger on the ass of one of the women before at last turning his full attention to his Alpha.

She gladly accepted the champagne and took it down in one bubbly gulp.

He raised a brow. "I take that as a yes."

She sighed and shook her head, staring out over the sea of glamorous people. "I detest all of this." Not that she needed to tell her Beta that. They had both grown up together, and he knew her better than she knew herself. "Strider's at it again," she said tersely, keeping an eye out for him.

Jack growled. "If the prick wasn't an Alpha, I'd take his tasteless comments and shove them up his ass."

Breanna snorted. "I'd endorse that." She groaned, banging the back of her head against the wall. Her elegantly styled bun bore most of the hit, and a few strands of jet-black hair came loose to dangle around her face. Her hairdresser would weep, seeing how she was mistreating her "masterpiece." "He's not the first overly ambitious Alpha to try to make me his mate, and I'm sure he won't be the last." Breanna gave Jack a reassuring, if not weary, smile. "Don't worry. I can handle him."

"I know you can." His arm brushed hers, a comforting, strong presence. And his way of reminding her he was always there for her if she needed him.

She took his hand and squeezed it, letting him know that subtle reminder meant more to her than words could express.

"How's the schmoozing with the new Beckinridge Alpha coming along?" Jack said.

Ah, the restless world of pack politics. Not one of her favorite topics, but one she was comfortable talking about at least. "It was going well, actually—until Strider strode up to him and began acting like we were a couple. He went on and on about how much he's helped me out over the years from behind the scenes while my father was still Alpha. Which we all know is a bunch of bullshit. He's never lifted a finger to help us." Her words stiffened as her jaw clenched. "What he doesn't seem able to understand is that the weaker he tries to make me seem, the more determined I am to get rid of him for good."

Jack's hand froze. It had been on its way to deliver the last bit of champagne in his glass to his very sensuous lips. "You mean, you're thinking about offing him?"

"If it comes down to it." She wasn't above murder to protect her pack, even if it was taboo for one Alpha to murder another. "He kept bringing up the recent rogue witch attacks in our territory. I haven't told him about them, which means he either has someone in the DPI on his payroll, or he had something to do with them."

"To prove his point. About you being too weak to protect your pack."

"My suspicions exactly. He also mentioned something about me 'not being strong enough to withstand the darkness in the coming war.' What the hell does that even mean?"

"No clue." Jack's brows furrowed, and he frowned. "I'll

see what I can find out."

"Thank you." She gave him a grateful smile. "I don't know what I'd do without you."

That turned his frown into a grin, and those heart-melting blue eyes of his sparkled with pride… and something else she couldn't quite name.

Actually she could, but she didn't want to. Didn't want to wreck things between them when their relationship was rock-solid. Given recent events, her pack's trust in her ability to protect them from outside threats was damaged. While her relationships with the majority of her pack members were intact, there were an alarming number of them who were beginning to doubt her ability to be a strong-enough Alpha to lead them. And they weren't shy about expressing those doubts to whomever would listen.

"You're too soft hearted. There's no place in a pack for an Alpha like that. You'll get your packmates killed, which is the greatest offense an Alpha could commit."

She'd heard her father's voice in her head often throughout the long, lonely years she'd been Alpha, constantly reprimanding her when she demonstrated sympathy or showed mercy. A man with little compassion, Bear Whiteclaw had been a force to be reckoned with in his glory days. She still couldn't believe he was dead. A mixture of grief and rage slammed into her, making her inner wolf growl.

The wolf who'd killed him had gotten away. When she'd walked in on her father's body, the air had been filled with blood. And the scent of wolf, pine, snow, and earth, a sharp, masculine smell that had forever been burned into her nostrils.

Shadow. That was the name of the wolf who'd killed her father. Had run a knife across his throat while he'd slept, and left him to bleed out.

Shadow had been apprehended by the DPI and tried for murder, but the charges were eventually dropped. The organization Shadow worked for wasn't the only one who'd wanted her father dead. She knew he'd committed some pretty underhanded acts to get where he was, but she had no idea as to the extent of his atrocities.

Her father had been evil, pure and simple.

But he had still been her father, her only living relative.

Blinking back tears, she straightened and cracked her neck. Her body felt tenser thinking about that night of blood and death. She needed a distraction. Anything not to think, not to feel. Otherwise, the rage might consume her.

"I'm going to find the ladies room," she said. "Then I suppose I'll drink more liquid courage and see if I can—"

The smell hit her as if she'd smacked into a brick wall. A mix of pine and snow, a reminder of loss and heartache.

Whirling, she murmured, "It can't be." Her eyes searched the crowd, tracking the scent. Distantly, she heard Jack say her name. She hadn't realized she'd started walking, following the scent, until the crowd parted and there he was.

The man who had murdered her father.

Shadow felt her watching him before he saw her.

His eyes followed his senses, locking onto a tall raven-haired woman with olive skin. Her eyes were slanted and deep brown, her brows thick and black, her lips full. Her features made her look like an Indian princess. Tribal tattoos of black ink covered her biceps and wrists in bands. The simplicity of her inky dress complemented the turquoise stones dangling from her ears. She was radiant.

And pissed as hell as she stormed over to him.

He raked his brain, trying to figure out who this woman was.

"How dare you show your face here, murderer!" she screeched, getting right in his face. Anger seethed from every pore in her lovely, toned body. Not that he was looking.

Eyes upward, mate.

He didn't flinch at the flung insult. He'd been called worse.

Drake stepped up to stand beside him. "Breanna," he said smoothly, ever the diplomat. "I see you've met my new head of security, Sh—"

"I know who he is," she spat, still glaring at him. "He's the man who murdered my father."

Stunned silence followed the statement. It was the first time Shadow had seen Drake struck speechless. A crowd had gathered around them as people pretended to be chatting but were secretly listening to the fight.

Freaking rubberneckers.

Drake at last shook his head and cleared his throat. "I'm sorry, you must be mistaken."

"No," Breanna said coldly, holding Shadow's gaze. The

burning fire in her eyes only made her more attractive. Breanna… Breanna… why couldn't he remember who she was? "I'll never forget the face of the man who killed Bear Whiteclaw."

Bear White… Oh fuck.

This was his daughter? Shadow remembered seeing her at his trial, giving a passionate testimony that nearly had the jury ruling in favor of killing his ass. He hadn't recognized her. She'd changed in the years since they'd met. She'd grown more into a woman.

A harder, colder version of the tearful pup mourning over her father, a man who deserved to rot in hell for the crimes he'd committed against mankind and paranormals alike. Killing Bear Whiteclaw had been doing the world a favor. Instead, it had earned him the scorn of a lot of people, including the fiery female in front of him.

Words of apology dried up in his mouth. How did you say you were sorry for something like that? "Miss, I—"

"What? You're sorry? Don't you dare lie to me, you son of a bitch." Her dainty hands formed fists, which trembled at her sides. Blood dribbled between her fingers, dripping to the floor. Her claws must have come out. He'd bet his retirement she was itching to tear his face off. She'd probably smile while doing it.

A tall blond man who looked as if he could bench press a bus walked up to Breanna and whispered something in her ear. The tension eased out of her, but only slightly.

She stepped up to Shadow, her lips brushing his cheek and making him shiver.

"If it's the last thing I do," she whispered, "I'll kill you."

In one fluid motion, she was gone. He watched her walk away, his body too wired from the heat burning through him.

A fire that had blazed to life the second her lips had caressed his skin with the threat of death.

CHAPTER FOUR

DAMN. THIS. FEVER. TO. HELL.

Shadow clenched his hands as he reined in his burning desire to go after the woman and do something he'd likely regret.

He tapped his foot as Drake turned to face him. "I knew you'd killed some pretty prominent figures in the Underworld," said Drake, still sporting the stunned look, "but I had no idea Bear Whiteclaw was one of them."

Shadow remembered Whiteclaw. Vicious bastard. His idea of fun had been to blackmail and cheat innocent people into doing what he wanted. Sometimes that resulted in his victims' deaths, especially if they did not comply. Whiteclaw had also believed in child labor. The Black Moon Pack had shut down more than one of his illegal operations. Shadow would never forget the sunken cheeks and hopeless gazes of the neglected children they'd saved.

Nor would he ever forget how pissed off that sad sight

made him.

Breanna had to know about the labor camps. But if she did, why the hell would she still defend her "father's honor"?

"Excuse me," he murmured to his Alpha, not waiting for a dismissal.

Drake sighed and muttered something along the lines of, "Cocky bastard. Walks off all the time without asking for permission…"

Shadow kept walking. His eyes tracked the female—and her delicious scent of jasmine and lilies—through the crowd.

He watched the lean muscles of her back work. God, the back of that dress was spectacular. As if a firework made of diamonds had exploded and formed straps. He also appreciated how low-cut it was.

Heat built within him. He felt the crotch of his pants tighten as he began to harden.

Damn. He should turn around now. But he kept walking, unable to stop until he reached her.

She sensed him before he could grab her. So had her bodyguard. Murder danced in the man's eyes as he strutted toward Shadow. Breanna held up a hand, and the bodyguard halted. She whirled around to face Shadow. Those lovely brown eyes blazed with fury. "You have a lot of nerve following me."

Beautiful. Absolutely beautiful.

Her own eyes appraised him, widening slightly. Some of the anger drained away.

His heart stuttered as he caught a whiff of desire

rolling off of her.

Keeping his expression neutral, he said, "Do you know what Bear did?"

"Excuse me?" That pissed-off look was back. Her eyes, which had been looking at his manhood, snapped back to his face. "Of course I know. I'm not proud of his many crimes. God, who would be? But he was also my father. You took away the only family I had left."

That had to be hard. And he could relate. His own family had been a far cry from perfect. It had still hurt like hell when he'd lost them. He'd never felt more alone in his life until then.

"Who's in charge of the Whiteclaw Pack now?" he asked.

Outrage sparked in her lovely eyes. Which he seemed unable to stop staring into. "Who the hell do you think, asshole? I am! We're one of the few packs that still passes the role of Alpha down through family."

Some old bloodlines—Crescent, Whiteclaw, and a handful of others—still functioned more like a monarchy. He also didn't know whether finding out she was an Alpha made her hotter or more intimidating. He decided on a little of both.

Without thinking about it, he took off his jacket.

Breanna took a step back. "What are you doing?"

Silently, he rolled up his shirtsleeve. Both arms were covered in non-matching tattoos and scars, as were his chest and back. He pointed to one tattoo in particular.

Her eyes followed and froze. "That's my family crest," she whispered.

"Whiteclaw," he said, pointing to the others. "One for every life I've taken."

"But why would you do that?"

"Because I want a reminder of what kind of a monster I am," he said without flinching, holding her gaze. "Every life I've taken has killed a part of me I'll never get back. The ink... it's cathartic. It eases the burden of the guilt somewhat."

Her lip rolled up in disgust. "Of course. You were doing this for yourself all along." She turned to walk away.

Dammit. How did he manage to fuck this up?

He donned his jacket and went after her. "That's not it."

"Oh? Because all I see is a self-absorbed killer tailing me."

He couldn't resist. "If I'm tailing you, how can you see me?"

Her heels screeched to a halt. Slowly, she turned.

He tensed. Uh-oh.

Wham!

Her palm flew across his face. He never saw it coming, she was that fast. And holy fuck, she hadn't held back. His cheek sang from the impact.

"What the—?"

Blue light flared from the back of the hand Breanna had used to slap him. Her jaw dropped in horror as the light faded. An indigo crescent-moon-shaped tattoo now lay etched in her skin.

Her mouth opened and closed several times before she spoke. "You-You asshole! You Marked me!"

This couldn't be happening. Surely, this was a nightmare, and she'd wake up any minute now. Or maybe someone had spiked her drink, and she was hallucinating. Because there couldn't possibly be a Mark on the back of her hand.

No, no, no, no, no...

Snatching a napkin off a nearby table, she began rubbing furiously at the Mark. And immediately felt stupid. Of course it wasn't coming off. It would remain inked onto her skin whether or not she decided to go through with the mating.

And oh, did her body want to.

She wasn't prepared for the wave of lust that swept through her upon seeing Shadow. He had always been attractive in a bad-boy, hands-off kind of way. But the black suit somehow accentuated his dark beauty and stoked her desire. Her craving for him had burned through her hatred and made her wonder dangerous thoughts. Loving him could destroy her. Letting him into her heart meant forgiving him, which she'd sworn never to do. He wasn't worthy of her forgiveness, not after everything he'd done.

Shadow stood nearby, eyes wide and speechless.

His silence was irritating. "Well," she snapped, "say something!"

Jack kept quiet behind her, watching the two of them. His body was tensed, as if he were preparing to break up a fight.

She almost wanted to start one. Wanted the chance to dig her claws into Shadow's flesh and make him bleed.

How *dare* he Mark her. She didn't need this right now, not when she was trying to evade Strider and keep her pack from mutinying.

Anger simmered in Shadow's lovely gray eyes. They reminded her of storm clouds. "What do you want me to say?" he asked with quiet fury. "You know as well as I do that I have no control over the Marking. Believe me, if it were up to me, I'd never Mark anyone."

She blinked. Why did that hurt? It shouldn't, not when she'd sworn to loathe him for all eternity. But it felt bitterly like a rejection. And if there was one thing she didn't handle well, it was being cast aside. "Well, don't worry," she said through gritted teeth. "You'll get your wish because I have no intention of ever going through with this mating."

"Wait," he said, catching her wrist when she turned to stalk off. "We should discuss this."

A demand, not a question. From a lowly pack wolf to an Alpha.

Who the hell did this guy think he was? It wasn't the first time she'd been bossed around by men who didn't hold her rank but somehow thought because she was a woman, she was weaker. Most of the time, she just let it slide and rolled her eyes. But for some reason with him, it only pissed her off more.

"Let go of me," she said, her voice a low growl. "Right. Now."

He did. The second he lifted his palm, she immediately missed his touch.

Which was fucking stupid.

Dammit. She didn't trust herself around him. Not

when her body was screaming to let him take her right now while her mind begged her not to. As for her heart... well, her emotions were such a convoluted mess right now that she didn't know who the hell's side her heart was on.

She needed to get out of here, away from him. Go somewhere where she could calm down and logically sort through all this.

"I need some air," she muttered. "Just go away. Forget you ever saw me." She ran, pushing through the crowd without apology and ignoring the burning wish that he would follow her.

And the sting of disappointment when he didn't.

CHAPTER FIVE

SHADOW STOOD THERE LIKE A STATUE. HIS UNBLINKING eyes followed Breanna—his mate—through the crowd until she vanished from sight.

What the hell was wrong with him? He should go after her, but he couldn't move. It was as if his body had suddenly turned to stone.

And why, exactly, did he feel the need to go after her? He should heed her warning. To go away and forget he ever saw her. Life would be a hell of a lot easier if he were never able to fall in love. She would be dodging a bullet by not mating a wolf whose paws were stained crimson.

But the thought of never seeing her again made his chest ache. The thought was unbearable. Unacceptable.

Snap out of it.

He started to walk in the direction she'd taken off, when a cool voice said, "You want some advice?"

That was right. Breanna hadn't been alone. In the heat

of the moment, he'd forgotten about Malibu Ken. The model-esque bodyguard stood a few feet away. He was leaning against a table, with his arms crossed and a pissed-off jut to his lower lip. Like a pup who was pouting about another pup taking away his favorite toy.

"How long have you been in love with her?" Shadow asked, countering with a question of his own.

Malibu stared at him, blinked, and then looked away. "It doesn't matter. Not anymore, now that she's been Marked by you."

Yeah, those last two words hadn't sounded bitter at all. Yet one more person who'd likely be out to kill him.

Get in line, pal.

"I never asked for this, either," Shadow said.

The guy snarled. "Marking her would be an honor. You make it sound like a burden."

"Because it is! I have enough on my plate without having to worry about a mate who wants to take my head off."

"Well, aren't you a knight in shining armor," he drawled, his voice dripping venom. "Maybe I'll save her the trouble and kill you myself."

"That would be ill-advised, Jack. Do you really want to doom your Alpha to a lonely existence, never able to fall in love?"

An elderly man with a fluffy gray beard and sharp blue eyes approached, leaning against an elegant, polished cane of black wood.

Shadow's eyes narrowed as he studied the stranger. His limp was faked, and the cane was likely a prop. Part of a clever disguise to make him seem feebler than he was, so as to catch opponents off guard. The pin attached to his tuxedo lapel marked him as the Alpha of the Montreal Pack. Which would make him...

Shadow immediately went on the defensive. "Captain Mark."

"Please, just Mark will do. No one's called me captain since my naval days." Despite the fact that he was approaching his seventies, the man's eyes were clear as day, sparkling with sharp intellect.

Which made him all the more dangerous.

Annnnnddddd.... just look at him. Not even thirty and paranoid as fuck. Hell, whom was he kidding? Mating was absolutely out of the question. He'd never be able to have a successful relationship ever because he'd always be wondering if the woman was out to get him. He didn't trust people. Couldn't trust them. The fuck-ups of his past had scarred him for life. He'd seen sin, had seen what people who supposedly loved each other did to one another when money or power was involved. People could turn on you in a flash.

And his destined mate already hated him, but that had kind of been expected before he'd Marked her, given the sheer number of people who wanted a piece of him.

It still floored him that he'd Marked someone. He never thought he'd find a mate, someone to share his life with. The lonely part of his soul yearned for companionship, but he knew he'd damned his own happiness the moment he'd taken that first life for money. Bounty hunting was a cruel sport at times. You really did sell your soul to the devil when you signed the hiring contract.

Sometimes he wondered if he had a soul left.

Some semblance of politeness kicked in, and Shadow extended a hand. "Shadow," he said, shaking.

"I know who you are," Mark said, his laugh lines crinkling around his smile. He looked at Jack. "If you ask me, Breanna couldn't have found a more fitting mate. These are dire times, as you well know. Alliances are shifting. Alphas are making grabs at power. A powerful, well-known pack led by one of the few female Alphas out there, and unmated to boot?" He scoffed. "Breanna has had a target placed on her back since her father died."

Subtle hint to Shadow: It's your fault she's in danger. You owe her your protection.

"What does it matter to you?" Shadow asked coolly, crossing his arms. "How do I know you're not one of these power-hungry Alphas you just mentioned?"

Jack looked at him as if he were crazy. Hell, he half-thought he was. Had seen a shrink plenty enough to be certified, he'd bet.

Mark raised a brow. The werewolf, who was legendary for being a hardass and one stone-cold motherfucker to his enemies, likely wasn't used to being talked to in such a manner. Few wolves had the balls. "You're cautious. That's a good trait to have in a mate. But let me assure you, as godfather to Breanna, I have nothing but her best interests at heart." He smiled pleasantly at Jack. "Could you excuse us for a moment? I have business I'd like to discuss with your future Alpha."

Jack looked as if he'd rather slit Shadow's throat. With a scowl on his face, he nodded and stormed off.

Shadow knew it was unlikely the last time he'd do the insult song-and-dance with the lovesick wolf.

Mark gestured to an empty hallway. "Walk with me?"

"Don't see you giving me much of a choice."

Mark chuckled as they began to walk at a leisurely pace, away from the crowd. "I like you. You have street smarts. A lot of these old crows think they're savvy when it comes to the brutalities of the Underworld, but none can hold a candle to you. You have real-world experience, as my father called it. He was a captain in the navy himself, as was his father before him, and so forth. I come from a long line of naval officers."

"Something tells me you didn't pull me aside to spout off accolades about your family's military history."

"No, I suppose I did not." Mark stopped, as did Shadow. The old bat looked around and said in a hushed voice, "I need you to mate with Breanna so you can take out Strider."

"Why?"

"He's not just a threat to her well-being. He's been nipping at my heels for years, waiting for me to croak so he can assume leadership of my pack. He's one of the few Alphas who controls two packs."

"Two?"

"Remember the Austin Pack? Tiny little thing from the South that grew and grew under the radar until they were one of the wealthiest packs in the country. Strider, posing as a lone wolf, joined their pack and then challenged their leader. Slaughtered him and took his place. Then he mated that female Alpha from the Midwest. Also the leader of a prominent, wealthy pack. Made her living in the fashion industry, of all things."

Huh. Odd choice for a werewolf, but hey, he wasn't judging. He had made his living cashing in bounties, after all. Ruining lives and all that. Fashion sounded noble in comparison.

"Once they were mated, she died of a mysterious illness. He inherited the pack and has been on the hunt for more wealth and power ever since."

"So you're not just looking out for your goddaughter's welfare—you're looking out for your own."

He smiled. It was far too cunning. "I never said I wasn't. Can you blame me?"

Son of a bitch had a dark streak after all, just as Shadow had suspected.

Goddamn selfish royal werewolves.

He could play this game. In fact, he was a pro at being a self-absorbed prick. "What's in it for me if I help you?"

Mark blinked and chuckled. "I'm not surprised. Street smarts, I said." He ran a hand over his beard thoughtfully. "What do you need?"

"I don't want to lead a pack, that's for damned sure." The thought made his blood turn to ice. What if he got them all killed, just as he had his team? "But I'm also not going to abandon my mate. I'm not that much of an asshole."

"Then what do you want?" Mark was losing patience. The question was curter, more demanding.

"A favor, doesn't matter what, to be called in at any time."

Mark stared, weighing his options.

Shadow grinned, showing his fangs. "Or I'll just worry about making sure Strider doesn't hurt *my* pack, and say to hell with what he does with yours."

Those blue eyes narrowed. "Cold, too, I see. Another useful quality for an Alpha. Very well." He growled a sigh.

Someone didn't like the circumstances. Tough shit. Everything had a price, Gramps. Life had taught him that.

"In exchange for you taking care of Strider—and just to make sure we're on the same page, I'm talking permanently—I'll grant you any favor you wish, so long as it's within my power to do so. Obviously, if you ask to be made president of the United States, I might have some issues."

"No."

"…No?"

"No. It means, if I want to be president of the United States, you'd better find a way to fucking make it happen. No exceptions. A favor of my choosing means just that—I call the shots."

"But—"

"No ifs, ands, or buts about it. You're either in, or you're out. Which is it?"

Red colored Mark's face, making the gold in his narrowed eyes pop. "Do not toy with me, pup."

Shadow snorted. "Do you realize whom you're talking to?" He leaned in, lowering his voice to a growl. "I could kill you six ways with my right paw. We are alone in a hallway, removed from the crowd. No one would even hear you scream."

Fear flickered over Mark's eyes, which had abruptly

snapped to their blue hue again.

God, sometimes Shadow was glad his reputation preceded him.

"Fine," Mark growled, long and low. "We have a deal."

"Good." Shadow shook his hand, squeezing hard, to the point of bones breaking. "And just so we're clear—from this point on, this means I own you."

Breanna watched the couples dance, arms crossed and a scowl on her face. Thanks to her werewolf side, the gallon of champagne she'd consumed had done nothing but make her stomach hurt. Not even the tingle of a buzz could be felt.

The crown princess and a wickedly handsome man whooshed by. Breanna's eyes swept over the princess's body, which was fuller than ninety percent of the female wolves' in the room. Envy practically turned her skin green. It had always been tough for Breanna to put on weight. As a pup she'd been close to gangly, a tall beanstalk of a girl who got made fun of by the boys for the way she looked. When she'd matured and finally—finally!—started filling out, she'd been ecstatic. But her soft, feminine curves turned into hard, lean muscle.

"Let the supermodels and actresses be soft," said her father. "You are an Alpha. You will be a living weapon."

So he had fashioned her to his liking, putting her on a strenuous workout routine and controlling every aspect of her diet. It had taken years before she was able to eat or drink anything more than protein shakes, eggs, and water without feeling guilty. She still felt some guilt, especially at Thanksgiving. But she felt nowhere near as restricted by what was on the nutrition label as she once did.

Still... if she said she wasn't jealous of the princess's feminine curves and full bosom, she'd be lying. There was no way Breanna would be able to pull off a dress like the princess was wearing. In fact, clothes shopping was a bit of a chore. Nothing ever seemed to look right. There was barely a dip where her waist was; for the most part, her body was straight up and down. Including her chest and ass, to her chagrin. Unfortunately, this meant a lot of clothes hung about her lithe form as though she were a human coat hanger. No shape to see.

"Whiteclaw!"

Breanna's teeth gritted. No one had called her that but her father.

No one.

Her anger surged as Strider shoved his way through the crowd. At six foot four, he was as built as he was tall. His tuxedo was custom-made, of a rich, inky fabric. His green eyes reminded her of the forest, one of her favorite haunts. Admittedly, he wasn't hard to look at. Some might even call him handsome. She had thought so too, once.

Before he'd opened his mouth and she'd realized what an ass he was.

His brown hair, styled with a bit of gel, looked disheveled, as if he'd been running. Reaching for her, he grabbed one hand and then the other, eyes landing on the Mark. "So it's true," he breathed, still staring. A growl rumbled up his throat. "Who the hell does this bastard think he is, laying claim to my prize? You can't mate him. I won't allow it. You're mine."

Her brain short-circuited for a second. "Excuse me?" she said, jerking her hand back. "I'll do as I damn well please, as is my *right as an Alpha*."

"You can't be seriously considering this."

Was she?

Shadow was undeniably gorgeous. And given his reputation, she knew he had what it took to be an Alpha. But that was precisely the problem—his past was nothing but a miasma of death, blood, and sorrow. He'd killed people for money. And from the recounts of those who'd witnessed some of the murders, he'd enjoyed it. What kind of a future could she possibly hope to have with such a man? Where would he lead their pack?

God, what kind of father would he be? Did he even have a heart left?

Strider let his breath out in an exasperated sigh, rolled his eyes, and ran his hands through his hair. Maybe that was why it was so disheveled; he'd been on the verge of pulling it out. She rather liked the idea of him worrying himself to death. Key words being "to death." "Come on, Breanna," he drawled, looking at her sternly, the way a father would at a misbehaving pup. "You're smarter than this."

She would be the first to admit that when her patience was running thin or she was stressed out, she could be a brat. And just for the pleasure of getting under his skin and seeing him squirm more, she looked him in the eyes and said, "I think you just don't like feeling threatened."

Gold flickered in his eyes, like flames. "No one threatens me."

"Well, there's a first for everything," said a dark voice.

Breanna inwardly groaned. Hadn't she told him to go away?

But there he was, the man who'd haunted her dreams for so long. The man who'd destroyed her family.

She wasn't the only wolf to toss a glare in Shadow's direction. A long list of enemies—another strike against him. He could endanger her pack, endanger her, or their pups.

Shadow approached Strider with the easy swagger of a man who knows he's the big fish in the pond. Intimidating as hell, his dark presence filled up any empty space between Strider and Breanna as Shadow pointedly positioned himself between them. He stared at Strider and crossed his arms, becoming a living statue.

Breanna kept her mouth shut, sensing Strider's hackles rise. A trill of satisfaction zinged through her.

Though Shadow might score bonus points for not backing down to Strider when many would, she reminded herself that in no way made him more trustworthy.

Or likable. Even with those delicious, thick arms of his. She'd bet they were corded with veins, finely tuned muscles meant for pummeling people.

Or killing them.

Her lust dried up, though a shadow of heat lingered south of her navel.

Strider's anger was practically boiling his brain, it was so hot. She'd never seen him stare at anyone with as much malice and hatred as he now did Shadow, who didn't even blink. If anything, he looked bored.

"Who the hell do you think you are?" Strider said in a low voice, somewhere between wolf and man.

A few of the nearest patrons had turned to stare.

Breanna's heart started to race. No, no, they couldn't fight here. While male wolves were known to duke it out in public, one such public display would only serve to make her look weaker. Incapable of taking care of herself.

"I've got this," she said, stepping forward and digging her nails into Shadow's arm. God, it was just as hard as she'd thought. She wondered how it would feel bared…

Stop it.

"No," Shadow murmured after a moment of thoughtful silence. Those glittering gray eyes stared at Strider, narrowed, calculating. His mouth turned up at the corners in a faint smile. "I think Mr. Strider here needs to be taught a lesson."

Oh no.

"Shadow—" she said, but Strider's outraged cry drowned out her voice, cutting through the waltz the orchestra had just started up.

Strider grabbed a fistful of Shadow's shirt. "You have any idea who the fuck you're dealing with, pup?"

Shadow merely arched a brow, glancing down and back up. Frost had formed in his eyes. "Do you?"

"I'm going to rip your smart tongue out," Strider growled. "Then I'm gonna rip your cock off and—"

It happened in a blink. One second Strider was spouting threats punctuated with profanity, and the next

Shadow grabbed his hand and *squeezed*. Strider yowled and stumbled as his knees tried to buckle.

"Come along now." Shadow dragged Strider toward the garden entrance, keeping pressure on his hand. He smiled, a cold, feral grin that would make lesser men piss their pants. "Wouldn't want to be late to class."

People parted for them as Shadow dragged him outside and down the stone steps to the pebbled pathway weaving through row after row of immaculately trimmed hedges. Honestly, who needed this much shrubbery? Just imagine the upkeep. It all looked like one gigantic headache to Breanna, who trotted along after them, curious to see how this would play out.

She should intervene, stop him before Strider could get hurt. And she knew Strider would get hurt. Shadow's well-being didn't worry her in the least. Mostly because she didn't give a damn, but also because she knew beyond the shadow of a doubt he was a man capable of taking care of himself.

Here was a man who was a force to be reckoned with, the kind of man her father probably admired and would have been glad to call son.

If Shadow hadn't buried a knife in his throat first.

Actually, he'd probably given him bonus points from the grave for being that cold hearted.

The balmy air filled Breanna's nose, carrying the scents of approaching fall. Dust, sun-ripened leaves, freshly tilled earth. She loved it, relished the smell of nature. It was almost as delicious as the scent of Strider's fear.

You should intervene, her conscience urged.

Instead, she crossed her arms and watched as Shadow released Strider. They'd come to some sort of patio nestled within the garden. Benches of iron and wood sat like spectators along the patio's circular border. The brick used to make the patio was so red, she wondered if they'd be able to see the blood. And there would be some, she could feel it. Call it a gift from her father. Bear had been involved in so many fights, so many "schoolings in pain," as he'd called them, that Breanna had developed a sixth sense when it came to anticipating violence.

"All right, then," Shadow said, looking perfectly at ease. "Let's see how big and bad the wolf really is."

Strider lost it.

In a blur of snarls, claws, and fangs, he launched himself at Shadow.

It was no contest. Shadow made him look like a mall cop taking on a trained assassin. Shadow's practiced, silky moves deftly blocked Strider's unrefined punches and kicks. About thirty seconds had passed before Shadow yawned and decided to end this little brawl. If you could call it that. Strider hadn't landed a single blow, as far as Breanna could tell.

With a gouge to the lungs and an uppercut to his jaw, Strider went flying. He crashed into a bush, deflating the poor thing, and lay sprawled there until two of his boys came to help him up. His head rolled on his shoulders, as if he was having a hard time focusing on Shadow as they passed.

"You'll regret that," Strider slurred.

Then Breanna realized he was talking to her.

Her throat went tight as she watched him leave.

"You're welcome." Shadow walked by her without so much as a backward glance.

"Hey, wait a minute!" She jogged to catch up. "I didn't ask for your help."

"Sure looked like you needed it, though."

She stopped and glared at him. Her nails always had a tendency to turn into claws when she was mad, and she was piping hot. Her claws scraped her palms, cutting them, but she didn't care. "I'm not some damsel in distress who needs saving."

Shadow paused and threw her an amused glance over his shoulder. "I never said you were." His eyes slowly traveled over her body.

Her breath quickened, and her pulse throbbed with heat. *So not going to analyze that right now.*

"I don't need your help," she said again. "I don't need you."

Shadow's eyes narrowed imperceptibly, and that gorgeous mouth crept up in a knowing smile. He turned and stalked toward her, a predator on the hunt. "Is that so?"

"Yes." She would not turn. Not flinch, not blink. Not even when he came before her, barely an inch apart, so close she could feel his hot breath caress her face as he leaned in.

"But you want me."

She blinked several times. "I-I do not."

"You don't sound very convincing." His mouth drew closer.

Don't. Look.

Dammit, she looked. Her eyes dipped to his lips, which were parted. She could see his tongue. And wanted it to make her moan.

She licked her lips, which were suddenly very dry. Inhaled a breath. "I—"

He went still, watching her tongue flick over her mouth.

Then he took her.

CHAPTER SIX

THE FIRST THING HE THOUGHT WAS, Damn, she tastes divine. Like smoke and salt and sex and cherries.

The second thing was, *What the fuck are you doing?*

He should stop. Or at least throw on the brakes. But once his tongue dipped into her mouth and she groaned, he couldn't stop.

And the wolf inside him didn't want to. It wanted to mate, right here, right now, under the open sky, in front of bugs and animals and, to hell with it, even the party guests.

He backed her up against a hedge, hands tangled in her silky hair. Which, by the way, was just as soft as he thought it would be.

Her initial resistance gave way to passion as she succumbed to his mouth's demands. Her body was hard, and it turned him on more. He appreciated a woman who took care of herself. She was toned but not buff. His hands slipped from her hair—well, one remained looped up in it, because it was just so damn soft and hard to let go of completely, while the other slid down her body, exploring. Conquering. Claiming what was his with his scent.

Her tongue lapped at his, stroking and licking until he thought he'd come unglued. His roaming hand swept past the cascade of diamonds, sinking down the soft skin of her back and dipping inside the low dip of her dress. His palm cradled her ass and squeezed.

She cried out, looped a lengthy leg around his hips, and crooked her knee to inch him closer.

As if he needed any encouragement. He thrust his hips forward; they fit together so perfectly. He rubbed his throbbing cock, concealed by the seam of his pants, against her sex. She moaned deep in her throat, arching her back to angle her hips forward and frantically rub against him.

The friction, the heat, was almost too much.

Holy fuck, he wanted to make her come. To hear her screaming his name, feel those long red nails scoring his back, making him hers.

He didn't even know he'd wanted this until it was happening.

And, please, never let it end.

Which it abruptly did in, like, the next two seconds.

The spell broke the moment she jerked back. Breanna stared at him, stunned. Her lips were swollen from his kisses.

Neither of them breathed.

When the silence became awkward, he wetted his parched lips and said, "What's—"

Wham!

His head jerked to the side, his cheek cutting into his teeth with enough force to slice it. Blood, hot and metallic, drizzled into his mouth. His skin burned. It took him a moment to realize what had happened.

And when he did, he was piping mad.

The sound of the slap filled up the silence, which only seemed to amplify it.

It had sounded like a good idea at the time. At least, it had in her head. A way to defend her honor as a lady. Dramatic, like something out of a chick flick.

Then common decency had taken over.

"Oh my God," she breathed. Horrified, she stared at her hand. "I don't know why I just did that."

Shadow's jaw ticked. A rough outline of her hand blazed red against his face.

Oh shit. She gulped, actually gulped. She hadn't done that since she was a kid, done something she shouldn't have, and her father had called her first, middle, and last names, telling her to come and receive her punishment.

Shadow looked pissed, like tear-somebody's-limb-off kind of angry. "Was that really necessary?" he asked tightly.

She could tell he was trying to rein in his anger.

Please, please, please don't kill me.

"I-I'm sorry," she blurted. "I don't know what came over me."

He raised a brow, not in amusement but annoyance.

His eyes slid over her face, landing again on her mouth. Those slate-gray eyes turned stormy, hungry.

Her heart sped up at the thought of him kissing her like that again.

And what a kiss. She was no novice to worldly pleasures, but damn. Few men—actually, no men, come to think of it—had ever made all thought cease inside her brain with nothing but his tongue. And she was constantly thinking, worrying over her pack, figuring out how to form new alliances or repair old ones, and so on. She accepted it as part of being an Alpha. But the momentary silence, the brief reprieve from constantly putting everyone else's needs before her own, had been, well, wonderful. Addictive.

She craved more. Holy fuck, she actually craved more.

"I can't do this," she whispered as he started to lean in again.

His hands, one of which was still in her hair and the other on her ass beneath her dress, tightened their hold. "But you want to," he stated simply.

She swallowed. "So what if I do?"

"I bet you swore to forever loathe me. Fire and brimstone kind of stuff. Why the change of heart?"

"You weren't exactly giving me much choice when you were kissing me like that."

"Like this?"

"Stop, stop!" She untangled herself, with great effort because her body didn't seem to want to move, and put a healthy two feet between them. Clearing her throat, she crossed her arms, aware her nipples had pricked and were clearly visible through the silk of her dress. It was like trying to cover up a neon sign that said I WANT YOU.

His eyes lingered on her chest then lifted to her face. A slow smile spread across his lips. "Your scent says it all, babe."

Damn, he was right. The perfume of her desire was everywhere.

So was his. And it was driving her inner wolf insane with the need to rut, to mate, to claim.

To be whole.

She hadn't realized how empty she'd felt these past few months until this happened. Now, the absence of his hands on her skin, his mouth on hers, made her feel hollower inside. When was the last time she'd been with a man and actually *felt* something?

Realizing she wasn't going to come close to him again anytime soon, he sighed hard. "Look, obviously Strider isn't going to leave you alone. You need backup. And you know the rule—an unmated Alpha can't stay Alpha once her Blood Moon has passed."

Now, she felt like a damn shell. Her heart pitched to the bottom of her stomach, weighing her down to the earth.

Of course she knew, dammit. She wasn't stupid. But accepting that law meant admitting she needed him.

She was Breanna Whiteclaw, daughter of Bear Whiteclaw, one of the most-feared werewolves in the Underworld. And she would bend to no one or nothing, not even her own desires.

Her father... her father would never condone this

match. Ever. Not even from the grave. It would be like a slap in the face, mating the very wolf who had killed him. Many wolves in her pack had loved her father dearly, had been with him for decades. Mating Shadow might save her pack, or it might mean tipping them past the breaking point and damaging what few good relationships she had left between her and her wolves. No, this wasn't right. There had to be another way.

"There has to be another way," she murmured. But the more she thought it, the more hopeless she felt.

Still, her fire burned bright, hopeful, cunning.

She was a Whiteclaw. If anyone could figure out an impossible situation, it was her.

"Excuse me." She swept past him without a backward glance.

"Where are you going?" he called, irritated.

"To find a way to stop Strider, save my pack, and keep my Alpha-hood—without mating you."

CHAPTER SEVEN

ETAWAYGETAWAYGETFARAWAY.

Her silent mantra as she stomped through the crowd, fleeing the scene of a crime of passion.

Another groan. Another mutter. "What the fuck were you thinking?"

More mentally beating herself up for being so reckless. She was an Alpha. She'd weathered many full moons, when werewolves' sexual desires were at their peak, and had come out fine every time, no strings attached.

She'd been the one in charge, no matter what the male thought.

She'd been the one to end their sexcapades if things got too rough.

She'd also been the one to roughen things up a little if the guy was being a pussy, thinking he'd hurt her "delicate female frame." She was a werewolf, for goodness's sake. It wasn't as though she were going to break.

Control, control, control. Her father had drilled it into her head from the time she could walk to the time he left this world.

An Alpha must exercise control in every situation. And, above all, over one's body and mind.

Her mind wandered back to the garden, to the thought of Shadow's hands exploring her curves, of his demanding, almost violent, kisses that had set her blood ablaze.

His seduction was the perfect combination of sweet and spicy, walking the line between being too much and not enough. It was tantalizing. She wanted more.

Subconsciously, she licked her lips. A low ache began below her navel, making her thighs squeeze.

No, her brain said firmly.

But that was the thing about being told no. It usually made her want it more.

Her desire burned brighter, hotter, her inner wolf whining to return to what it knew was its mate.

Its mate.

Oh God. What was she thinking? She could never mate that man, that monster.

He had killed her father. Even if by some miracle they managed not to take each other's heads off during the mating ceremony, love could never grow between them with so much resentment and distrust holding them back.

She blinked. Since when had she wanted love to be part of the equation? Being nearly thirty, she'd assumed she'd never find her Blood Mate. Some wolves never did, and that was fine by her. One less person to be upset over when they left you… Like her father, her mother. Her friends, when she'd become Alpha, who'd let their envy drive them away.

She'd assumed, like many Alphas, that she'd never find her mate and would instead mate for mutual benefit. An exchange of coin, resources, power. A bond to strengthen their packs. She would produce pups if necessary, and love the hell out of them. They would never grow up feeling like a pawn or a weapon or as if they didn't matter as people. No, she'd never subject her children to what she went through. Hell would freeze over first.

Still… the thought of mating a stranger for strictly political reasons sounded so cold. She'd much rather snuggle her Blood Mate, relishing his warmth and love.

And for some reason that puzzled her, she could only picture Shadow in that position.

Instead of going to her room, she went to Jack's. She opened the door without preamble, aware by the paranormal signature crackling along her sixth sense that he was in.

And he wasn't alone.

They were on the bed—or what was left of it. Pillows, sheets, and down lay strewn about the room, as though a goose had exploded. Jack sat up on his knees, pants down around his ankles, taking a werewolf female from behind. And from the sounds of her moans and the claw marks on the walls, she was enjoying the hell out of it.

Breanna raised a brow, cleared her throat.

"What is it?" Jack growled over his shoulder then looked. "Fuck!"

"Yes," the woman breathed, "fuck me harder. Wait,

what the hell? Where are you going?"

Jack scrambled off the bed, nearly tripping as he yanked his pants upward.

Breanna angled her head, observed the bowtie still around his neck. "Ever consider auditioning for the Chippendales?"

Jack's face flushed crimson, and he looked away.

Breanna briefly admired the view of his naked abs and lean torso. He truly was beautiful.

Images of what Shadow would look like undressed paraded about her mind. Not that she had mentally undressed him earlier or anything.

Her eyes flicked to the fuming woman. "Leave us."

Growling, she wrapped the sheet around herself like a towel and stomped over to Breanna. "Who the hell do you think you are?"

Jack swore. The woman did too, when Breanna's hand found her throat, forcing her against a wall with enough impact to crack her skull.

"You're either very brave or very stupid to disobey an Alpha's orders," Breanna hissed in a low voice, eyes blazing gold. "And from the looks of you, I'm going with the latter. Now get out. While you're still able to draw breath."

The woman's knees nearly buckled when Breanna swiftly released her. Without another word, she hightailed it out of there, leaving behind tense silence.

Breanna shut the door and chuckled. "I see your taste has improved."

"What's it to you? You never cared whom I fucked before."

"Someone's testy. Care to talk about it?"

"No." He went to the minibar, poured himself a drink, and knocked it back. Poured another and did the same.

Breanna plopped on the bed and lay down against the rumpled bedsheet. It had a long gash down the middle, as did the mattress itself, exposing the coils and padding inside. She idly twirled a piece of wool between her fingers and flung it to the floor. "You're paying for this."

"I know."

"Have a seat. We need to talk."

He looked as if he'd rather drink battery acid than sit next to her. But he knew as well as she did that no one refused an Alpha's demands, not without consequences.

He sat down on the edge of the bed, body tensed as if expecting a secret attack.

She raised a brow but said nothing. "Strider knows about the Mark."

"Fantastic," Jack drawled with sarcastic flair. "He threatened to kill Shadow yet?"

"Actually, the other way around. Shadow left him with a magnificent black eye, and probably a bruised jaw, too."

"Well, I gotta hand it to him." He raised his glass and drank.

She snatched it away from him, set it on the nightstand. "What's with you?"

"Nothing outside of the usual." A sloppy grin.

A growl rumbled in her throat. "Don't patronize me. Tell me what's wrong."

"You really ought to work on your bedside manner." Pursing his lips, he sighed hard. Some of that tension deflated. "I feel like I'm losing you."

She blinked. "How?"

"Because for the longest time it's been you and me. I'm your Beta, your adviser. The shoulder you cry on when you cry—not that you do much," he added hastily at her glare. "But now it feels like I'm being, I don't know, replaced."

She laughed. "No one could ever replace you. Don't be silly, Jack."

"Well, you asked why," he said testily, getting up.

She grabbed his hand, stopped him. "I'm sorry. I didn't mean to laugh. Sit."

He did. Looked at her. Sadness gathered in his eyes.

She waited, held her breath.

"Is it selfish of me to have hoped you never found your mate?" Jack whispered. "That you'd someday choose to mate me?"

Breanna's heart skipped. Out of surprise, yes, but desire... not so much. Now that Shadow had entered her life, she wasn't sure she could ever view another man as his equal. Wasn't sure if she could ever feel the same about another man, period. "The thought... crossed my mind," she admitted. "But I thought you wanted no part of being an Alpha."

"I would have if you were my queen."

She gazed at the Mark on her hand. "It is what it is. I can't control the Marking, any more than Shadow can." Deep breath. "If you want to leave the pack, I'll—"

"No! God, no, I'll never leave you. I can't. You've been a part of my family for years now."

She smiled. "I'm glad you're staying. And I'm sorry I

cannot return your affection."

"I know." That devil-may-care smile reappeared. "Though you have to admit, I would have made one hot piece of Alpha man candy."

She snorted. "Did you just refer to yourself as man candy?"

"Yup."

She shook her head and giggled. "You'll never change. And I hope you don't."

"Ditto." He sighed in resignation and finally leaned back beside her. Their heads touched, and the intimacy warmed her. "You going through with it, then? The mating?"

"I don't know. It's… complicated."

"How?"

"What do you mean how?"

"I mean, I know he killed your father," he said gently. "No one can blame you for being sore about that. But you also have to remember that's in the past. You mating or not mating Shadow isn't going to bring your father back."

Her chest grew tight. "I know."

Jack drummed his fingers along his abs, deep in thought. "Shadow showing up is a blessing, if you think about it. Strider's been growing bolder and more impatient. His wooing of you is starting to get a little aggressive."

"I can handle him."

"I know you can. But it doesn't hurt to ask for help, either." He sat up and propped his chin on his palm, looking at her. "Strider isn't going to back down until someone puts him in his place. And Shadow has a rep for being one badass motherfucker. Much as I hate to admit it, I think he out-machos me."

"No way."

Jack grinned. "Yeah, only a little, but still. This goes back to what I was saying about him being a godsend."

"But he—"

"I know how much you hate what happened to Bear. I know how much you hate Shadow as a result of that. It was traumatizing, and you've got baggage. I get it. But as an Alpha, you should also realize by now you can't put your feelings before the pack's well-being. Strider will be hoping you reject Shadow. It's the perfect opportunity for him to take over your pack and steal your father's legacy. The only way to prevent this is to mate with Shadow."

That rock-in-the-stomach feeling returned. "You're right. About all of it. Strider is growing desperate. There's something else at play here, but I haven't been able to uncover his true motivation yet."

"You need to have motivation to be a professional asshole?"

She arched a brow.

"Kidding, kidding. Just trying to lighten the mood. You look like you'd rather be hit by a bus than mate Shadow."

"That doesn't sound so bad, in comparison."

He nudged her playfully. "Judging by that look on your face, it seems to me you already knew the answer to the Strider problem. You were just unwilling to embrace it."

She swallowed. A lump the size of Texas had formed

in her throat. "I don't know how to forgive Shadow. I don't know if I can."

He squeezed her hand. "Work on getting along first. Then see if the forgiveness comes more naturally."

"I don't want to mate him."

Jack's steely eyes gazed steadily back at her. "You're an Alpha. So suck it up and start acting like one."

Start acting like one.

She was whining. Whining like a child who didn't want to eat her peas or go to bed at a decent hour or get up for school. A little brat who wasn't getting what she wanted.

Tough shit, Breanna. She'd given up free will the second she'd sworn the oath as Alpha. To protect her pack above all else, even if it meant sacrificing her heart's desires.

It truly didn't matter what she wanted or didn't want to do—it mattered what was best for her people.

Her family, her brethren.

Her father's legacy.

She would be damned if she'd let Strider get his filthy, corrupt paws on them. Sure, Bear Whiteclaw hadn't been a model citizen by a long shot. But he had been damn proud of his pack and had looked out for their well-being no matter the cost. For her to do anything less would be a disgrace to her family name.

And realizing that somehow made the prospect of mating Shadow seem not so bleak. If anything it gave her hope, made her feel lighter.

But only a little.

Still, it was a start.

"Thanks, Jack. That's just what I needed to hear."

He nodded with a grunt. "Anytime. You know I'm here if you need me."

She sat up and did something she rarely did—she hugged him. Bear Whiteclaw had never shown her much affection growing up. She knew people hugged, saw it all the time with the members of her pack. Still, it felt awkward… but nice. A way to show her gratitude.

He tensed at first, but then his arms slowly wrapped around her, holding her close.

His scent, a seductive, musky cologne that reminded her of moonlight and darkness, was so familiar, comforting. Here, with him, she felt at home.

She'd been wrong to think the last of her family died with her father. Her family was right here, and back at home, where her pack awaited her return.

"Protect your family, Breanna," her father had said.

I promise, she thought. *I promise not to let any harm come to them.*

They at last parted. Breanna pressed her lips together and straightened out her dress while Jack cleared his throat, gave an awkward, curt nod, and stood. "I'm, uh, guessing the royal family won't appreciate me strutting around shirtless at a formal event. I'm gonna, um, get dressed."

Breanna grinned. "I'm sure a few of the lady werewolves wouldn't mind."

He laughed. "Yeah, but their mates might." He tugged on his white shirt, started to button it. "You know, I'm glad we got all this out in the open. I feel so much—" He froze, eyes darting to the windows, then the door. He sucked in a breath as Breanna tensed, listening and smelling.

The air had a faint ozone smell to it, like wiring burning after a power surge.

She sucked in a breath. "Magic. Someone's casting a—"

The next second, Jack dove for her, knocking the breath from her when they hit the floor as gunfire shattered the windows.

It had taken Shadow nearly half an hour to calm down. And even then he wasn't anywhere near calm. He'd just forced himself to get back inside and attend to his Alpha like a good little bodyguard.

Shadow approached Drake, who turned to him with an amused smile and the glitter of a laugh in his eyes.

"Sorry, sir," Shadow began, "but I—"

"Marked someone? I heard."

Not surprising. Drake knew everybody's business. He was like Google personified.

Drake looked around. "Where is your mate?"

"She's… not warming up to the Marking."

"Whiteclaw, correct?"

"Yep."

"Fuck."

"Yeah. My thoughts exactly."

He sighed. "Don't worry. She'll come around. She'll have to."

Shadow snorted. "'Don't worry, Shadow. You'll get the

girl. She will have to mate you by default, after all, if she wants to remain an Alpha.'"

"I didn't mean it like that."

"I know. Doesn't make it any less true."

Which sucked. He shouldn't have come here. Shouldn't have thought he could live a halfway normal life without fucking up anyone else's.

The words "I quit" burned on his tongue. It wasn't the first time he'd thought about resigning. Thought his Alpha would be better off for it. But leaving Drake and his pack meant abandoning his crew. Sometime over the past few months, they'd become his family. Or as close to one as he was going to get. Though he distanced himself from them, he begrudgingly admitted he looked forward to their company. He saw it now that he might have to leave them.

And work had become fun again. Here, with a gun strapped to his hip as the sharks circled… he was in his element. It charged him, filled him with purpose. If anyone ever had a calling to be a badass, it was him.

Still… there was the problem of what he would do with this job if, by some miracle, Breanna decided to go through with the mating. He couldn't very well lead a pack and work as a Beta and bodyguard for another. That shit wouldn't jibe with Breanna. She was the type of wolf to demand a man's full attention—as she should. She was an Alpha, as he would be if she chose him.

Chose him. As if he had already made the decision to accept the mating. Which he hadn't, at least, not consciously.

Fuck. What the hell was he going to do?

He went into "his zone," as he always did whenever he was thinking too hard. All the background noise had blended to a low hum—the sound of Drake's laughter, the chatter of the patrons, the lilt of the waltz strummed by the orchestra. The clink of heels, the sweep of silk, the whisper of bullets being loaded into a—

His breath caught. "Get—"

Gunfire split open the cheerful atmosphere. Screams rang out, sounding tiny against the blast of the gunshots.

He dove for Drake, pinning his Alpha to the ground and shielding him with his body. His mind wasn't on Drake, though—it was on Breanna.

His eyes scanned the frantic crowd, searching for her raven-black hair and those outstanding diamond straps on her dress that he'd so badly wanted to snap off to expose more of her silky skin.

Sir! His second-in-command, via telepathic pack-link. *Brent's gone after one of the gunmen. We're pulling the car around right now.*

Meet you out front.

The gunfire abruptly died as the royal guards seized control of the situation. The interior artistry of the castle had been demolished. Vases and flowers lay shredded on their pedestals. Wallpaper, stucco, and tapestries had been chewed up by a barrage of bullets. It was a shame, really. All this finery, laid to waste.

Giving the foyer and surrounding rooms one last visual sweep for Breanna, Shadow forced himself to focus on the task at hand. Hauling up his Alpha, he rushed him to the front steps.

Bronx greeted him. "A few people were hit in the attack. Nothing major. All of them will live. They say the High Family were the targets."

"What?" Drake said. "Is anyone hurt?"

"The queen. She's been shot."

A curse followed.

"All the more reason to get you out of here," Shadow said. "The High Family might have been the targets, but other royals could potentially be as well." He passed Drake off to Bronx, who swiftly led him to the car. Shadow followed.

"We had Natalia do a scan of the vehicle for any explosives, just in case someone got the bright idea of planting one on it in the parking lot," Bronx said. "She's done a sweep of the area, too. We're all clear."

Damn. Shadow loved the shit out of some magic sometimes. He hadn't been too keen on hiring a witch at first, but on Bronx's suggestion, he had. And it had paid off the numerous times she'd saved their lives with her arsenal of spells, charms, and wards. "Good move. We should get him out of here as soon as possible." People were rushing past them in droves, running for their lives—and their cars. Though the attack was clearly over and the guards were in charge, it didn't stop the onslaught of panic that had many patrons stampeding down the steps like a herd of frightened antelope.

Bronx froze, listening. Someone must have been contacting him telepathically. "That was Brent. The gunman he went after was killed by palace guards. The other two got away. They were all warlocks, and they were using enchanted bullets."

"Enchanted? For what purpose?"

"They aren't sure yet. They sent the bullets off to be tested."

"Hmmm… At any rate, we should get Drake out of here, in case there are other attacks and this was just the first wave."

"Yes, sir."

He went to join their party in the waiting car. Two more cars would follow, with a third leading the way, in case there was trouble on the road.

Shadow went to climb inside the limo—to find the doors were locked. He tried the handle again. The fuck?

The window rolled down. Drake reached a lazy hand out and unfastened the insignia pinned to Shadow's lapel.

The one that marked him as a member of Drake's pack.

"What the hell are you doing?" Shadow demanded.

Drake chuckled. "Only you would talk to your boss like that. I'm letting you go."

"What? Why?"

"You're worried about her. Your mate. Your fear for her is stifling. Go to her."

"I… That is, sir—"

"You Marked someone. Another Alpha. The law says I cannot keep you. She is your priority, your responsibility now. Guard her well. Be safe, my friend. I hope you find happiness."

The window rolled up. The next second the limo drove off, leaving Shadow standing on the castle steps, dumbfounded.

CHAPTER EIGHT

THE GUNFIRE WAS CLOSE ENOUGH TO RATTLE BREANNA'S eardrums, teeth, and bones.

The attack felt as if it lasted an eternity but in truth had been over in less than a minute. When it stopped, neither she nor Jack moved right away. They lay there for a minute after the gunfire stopped, smashed against the floor. Waiting, listening, not daring to breathe for fear they'd miss something.

And the entire time, all Breanna could think about was if Shadow was injured or worse. She wasn't sure which unsettled her more—the idea that someone was shooting up the castle or her worrying about the welfare of a man she supposedly despised.

At last, Jack pulled her up. He silently finished getting dressed, not needing to be told they were about to head downstairs. "I'll go," he said. "You stay here, for your own safety."

She put a hand on the door, preventing him from opening it. "It's sweet you're trying to be a protective little Beta, but I'm not going to sit up here and hide like some princess in a tower while her knight fights for her honor. I'm going with you."

He didn't argue, having learned long ago he'd never win.

The two of them headed downstairs, where things were hectic. The noise swelled as the guards directed people to safety and tried to keep them calm.

The castle was a wreck. Glass from the many shattered windows lay scattered about the floor along with demolished vases and other fine décor. Bullet holes pockmarked the walls, and shredded tapestries blew in the wind that now leaked through the blown-out windows.

Breanna's eyes immediately scanned the crowd for her mate.

Her mate.

Since when had she started thinking of him as such?

Since the moment you thought you'd lost him, and your heart stopped beating.

Swallowing past the hard knot that had formed in her throat, she wove through the crowd.

A heavy sigh came from behind her, right before a warm hand took hers and turned her around. "Thank God. There you are. I've been looking all over for you."

She was too stunned to speak. Shadow pulled her to him, clutching her to his chest in a fierce, protective hug. His hard body radiated warmth and strength. She sniffed—no blood that she could smell. He must not have been hit.

Her body relaxed slightly.

An image of her father, drenched in blood, flashed through her mind. Mood officially killed. She pulled back and crossed her arms before looking away.

Shadow's arms stayed in place a moment longer before falling at his sides. He looked at Jack. "Thank you for keeping her safe."

"It's my job, as her Beta," he said tersely.

"Jack," Breanna murmured. *Not now,* she said through their pack-bond.

The golden glow in his eyes vanished, but she could still sense that his inner wolf's hackles were raised.

Wolves will be wolves.

Shadow paid him no mind, not seeming worried in the least. If his earlier throw-down with Strider in the courtyard was any indication, he could decorate these walls with Jack's insides if he tried to start something.

Breanna stepped in between them, just in case.

Shadow's eyes flicked from her to Jack and back to her again. "My sources tell me there were three gunmen. One of them was killed. All of them were warlocks, using enchanted bullets."

"What did they want?" Jack asked.

"They were after the High Family, so far as we can tell. There's a unit sweeping the grounds by foot and by air to scan for more assassins."

"Or terrorists," Jack muttered.

She looked at Jack, eyes narrowed in thought. *You think they're linked to the witch attacks on our pack and around the country?* she said to him on their private link.

Possibly. Guess we won't find out unless they catch them.

"What are you guys talking about?"

They both looked at Shadow.

He pointed between them. "I can tell you're doing your telepathic pack-link thing. And seeing as I've Marked your Alpha…"

Breanna gulped. He had a point. Though she still had no idea whether or not she was actually going to go through with the mating ceremony, he technically had a right to know about pack affairs now that he'd Marked her. "There have been… attacks recently on my pack."

Those steely eyes became colder. "Attacks? By whom?"

"Witches," Jack supplied. "So far as we can tell."

His brow arched. "You've been attacked multiple times?"

"Seven, to be exact," Breanna reluctantly admitted, keeping her voice down. She glanced about; it didn't appear that anyone was listening. Knowing a pack was under attack, and probably stressed as hell from it, was exactly the kind of dirt these bastards and bitches wouldn't hesitate to use to their advantage. And a pack-war wasn't something Breanna had the resources to tackle right now. "They've all happened within the past three months, shortly after word spread like wildfire about the witch attacks around the country."

Shadow's sensuous lips pressed together in a thin line. "Tell me everything."

Thirty minutes later, she'd done just that. After slipping away to one of the undamaged drawing rooms and locking the door, the three of them had sat down, and Jack and Breanna had revealed everything.

"The attacks started out small at first," Breanna said, still afraid to speak too loudly even though they were in a private room. Wolves had awfully good hearing; she swore sometimes they could hear through walls. "My father was big into working the land to provide what we needed. Our pack relies on our farms, both for food and for business. He had his paw in just about every food business throughout the world." She wetted her lips. The bottom one was quivering, as it usually did anytime she had to refer to her father in the past tense. "Anyway, like I said, it was small stuff. All the eggs in the henhouse would be smashed, or a portion of our crops would be demolished. It always looked like wild animals had gotten onto our land and caused mischief. Then one day we came home to find our entire crops burning."

"Burning?"

"All ten thousand acres of it," Jack pitched in. "Breanna and I were getting back from a business deal with a neighboring pack. We could see the smoke from over twenty miles away."

"Jesus," Shadow breathed, crossing his arms and stroking the stubble along his chin. He swore doing so helped him think better. "So I'm guessing by the grim looks on both of your faces, things got worse?"

"Oh yeah," Jack went on. "All our cattle was slaughtered next. Looked like something for a ritual. Gave me the heebie-jeebies. I still have nightmares about it."

"Next, there was what the authorities believed to be a carbon monoxide leak in part of our pack home from a 'faulty' furnace," Breanna said.

"But you don't believe it was caused by the furnace."

"No," Breanna said firmly with a shake of her head. "I've always had a strong 'gut instinct.' And mine told me the furnace wasn't responsible. So I hired a witch, and she managed to find a rather cleverly crafted spell meant to mimic carbon monoxide and its effects. It also made it appear as if the furnace had caused the problem without giving away any signs of someone actually physically tampering with it."

"We turned in our findings to the DPI. They revisited some of the attack sites, using our freelancing detective witch to help them. She found that same magical residue at all the other sites," Jack said. "Though whoever cast the spells was so good at covering their tracks, the DPI's crime lab couldn't find much to help us identify the culprit or culprits. They attributed the attacks to the same rogue witches who've been wreaking havoc around the nation."

Shadow grunted. "Whoever came to that conclusion was probably at the end of his shift and just didn't want to do any real work. The Department of Paranormal Idiots—I mean, 'Investigation'—isn't exactly known for hiring the most hard-working of individuals."

Jack and Breanna looked at one another.

"What is it now?" Shadow prompted.

More lip biting. "About a week after the carbon monoxide incident," Jack said quietly, "one of our pack members was killed while out on perimeter patrol."

"Killed? How?"

Breanna's hands shook. "He… He was…"

Jack clasped her hand. "He was relieved of his skin."

"Holy fuck." A few other curses whipped through his head, but he held them in. "I'm guessing there was magical residue on his body, as well?"

Breanna winced at the word "body." Shit. Shadow made a mental note to be gentler. Obviously, it was a topic that upset her, and rightfully so. No Alpha worth his or her title ever wanted to see harm come to their pack.

"Yeah," Jack said, leaning back in his chair. His foot had begun to tap. "It was similar to that left behind from the carbon monoxide spell. It had the same signature."

"Only one?"

"Yes."

"So likely only one witch or warlock was responsible for this."

"That's what it looks like," Breanna said. "But to cause that much destruction… What kind of witch or warlock could wield that kind of power? With that level of skill?"

Jack took a deep breath, let it out. "People are scared. A few have even asked to leave the pack, but Breanna refused, saying they are more vulnerable away from the safety of the pack."

"At which point they responded that they didn't appear to be very safe there either," Breanna said, not without ire. "They're losing their faith in me."

"Do you know anyone with a grudge against you? Anyone who might try to do you harm?" Shadow asked.

Breanna regarded him coolly. "As you're well aware, my father had many enemies, people who wouldn't hesitate to do me harm just to spite him, even though he's six feet under. But the one man who has blatantly shown interest in my pack would be—"

"Strider," Shadow finished. "He's trying to whittle down your pack's trust in you, make you appear weak. Then he can swoop in and save the day."

"Or challenge me for my title," Breanna said without batting a lash.

The thought of petite Breanna facing down that vicious asshole in a fight to the death made Shadow's blood chill.

But she didn't seem scared. Amelia hadn't either. His beautiful, strong baby sister. Brave until the end…

As he'd watched his former Alpha drive off in that limo, he'd made a promise to himself—to protect his new Alpha at whatever cost.

He'd failed his sister.

He'd failed his crew.

But he sure as hell wasn't going to fail his mate. He'd die first.

"Do we have any direct links to Strider?" Shadow asked.

"Nothing stronger than my gut instinct that he's involved," Breanna said grimly. "If he is, he's doing a good job of covering his tracks."

"He would have the money to hire a witch of that caliber," Jack said. "So it's not outside the realm of possibility. Plus, he's been trying to obtain the Whiteclaw Pack for years, though he seems to be getting more desperate."

"The question is, why?" Shadow murmured, thinking.

"Exactly what we'd like to know," Jack said.

Breanna stared at Shadow's lapel and frowned. "What happened to your pack sigil?"

"Hmmm?" Shadow looked down at his bared lapel. The pinholes where the pin had been glared back at him. "Oh. My Alpha, um, fired me," he mumbled.

"Sorry, couldn't quite catch that over the topic evasion," Jack said.

Shadow narrowed his eyes at him. "I said my Alpha fired me."

Breanna blinked. "Fired? Whatever for?"

Shadow's eyes met hers. "Because he says I belong to a new Alpha now. By law, he cannot keep me."

Breanna's face paled.

Jack nodded. "Makes sense. Guess this really means you're one of us, eh? A Whiteclaw." He leaned forward and slapped Shadow on the back. It would have looked friendly had Jack not subtly dug his claws into Shadow's suit, a reminder that he was always watching.

Shadow resisted the urge to grin. *Breanna has chosen her Beta well*, he thought not for the first time that night.

Breanna's lips pursed. With a huff, she said, "Fine. You can prove your worth by helping me take down Strider."

Shadow grinned. The hunter in him still got giddy at the possibility of fucking some asshole up. "It would be my pleasure."

CHAPTER NINE

STRIDER WAS BALLS-DEEP IN SHIT. NOT LITERALLY, OF course, but figuratively, which was almost worse. He just hadn't realized how deep he was in until he left his rooms to rejoin the party.

He'd just joined the crowd to find Breanna—or put a knife in that asshole werewolf Shadow's back—when gunfire rocked his world. He'd hit the floor so fast he'd knocked his temple against the cold marble. The world had blacked out for a minute then come back first in a blur and then into focus.

The marble beneath his body was so polished, it was like a mirror. Only his face wasn't the one reflected back at him.

It was Melaney's. And she looked pissed.

Startled at seeing the blond witch, he scrambled up. Bullets still rocketed through the air, but he didn't care. Getting shot up would be a mercy compared to what that sadistic bitch would do to him.

Racing down the hall and plowing through people scurrying to get away from the assault, Strider turned a corner—and was literally pulled *through a wall*.

He gasped at the prickling sensation along his skin, a sign magic was involved. Which, of course, it had to have been. No normal person, wolf or otherwise, could walk through walls.

He'd been pulled into an empty parlor. Well, almost empty. Melaney stood there, hands clasped calmly in front of her. She wore a lovely silk dress of deep purple; shimmering topazes dangled from her ears and wrapped about her throat and wrists. Her long blond hair hung freely around her shoulders in curly waves.

She was a knockout, Strider had to admit, even though he wasn't into witches. Power coupled with beauty, however, was awfully attractive.

Too bad she was scary as hell.

Those big blue eyes batted long, dark lashes at him. "Strider," she said in that low, seductive voice of hers that reminded him of molten chocolate, "I know you haven't been avoiding me intentionally since our last talk. Since you've been too busy to return my calls, I decided to come find you."

He gulped.

She smiled pleasantly at him, those ruby-red lips of hers glistening. "I know after I loaned you all that power you're not going to back out on our deal."

"Of course not," he snapped, though his inner wolf whimpered. Even it was afraid of her. "I've just been busy, as you said."

"Indeed." She angled her head to the side, studying him like a hawk about to swoop in for the kill. "Busy trying to obtain the Whiteclaw Pack, I hope, for our Mistress's use."

"Yes, very busy."

"Then why haven't you secured it yet?"

"I'm working on it. There have been... some snares."

"You're saying you can't handle the job?"

"Of course I can!" The very idea that he was somehow incompetent made his inner wolf growl. He kept it firmly leashed. The last time he openly growled at Melaney crossed his mind, making him shudder. He had no desire to repeat what had happened, to have his gut split open and magically sewn back together over and over again for his insolence.

Melaney smiled. The bitch seemed to live for getting under his skin. "Just checking. We wouldn't want to disappoint the Mistress. You never want to see her upset."

Hell, no, he didn't. For whatever reason, she seemed to have a penchant for making werewolves suffer.

"And just in case you're thinking of backing out of our bargain..." Melaney gripped his wrist and flipped it up. A pentagram of purple ink lay on his skin, shimmering faintly. Melaney tapped the Latin inscription at the pentagram's center with a black-lacquered nail. "Let me remind you this means 'servant.' And the Mark is permanent. Your fealty to our Mistress is forever." Her nails dug into his skin to the point of lancing flesh. His body tensed as she leaned in, lowering her voice. Her blue eyes blazed with purple flames. "If the thought of running and hiding from me so much as crosses your mind, I'll know, as I am the one who branded you for her. As generous as I've been with loaning you my power, I don't take kindly to betrayal."

He didn't dare flinch as she stared him down. She blinked and spun on her heel, dropping his wrist. Her delicate shoulder lifted in a shrug. "I can't imagine why you would consider backing out of the deal that could turn your life around, a once-in-a-lifetime opportunity to bail yourself out of all that debt. After all, Mistress has promised that in exchange for securing the Whiteclaw Pack for her, she will make you its Alpha. She's handing you the keys to the kingdom. You'd be foolish not to take her up on her offer. And even dumber to throw it back in her face. Think about it."

Her form rippled out of existence as she vanished.

He felt the remnants of her vast power long after she left. Five minutes later, after he'd sunk down into the deep cushions of a sofa, the hairs all along his body still stood at attention.

God, he could use a drink. A thorough search of the room told him there was no alcohol to be found here. Which meant rejoining the party to find booze, but he was in no mood to deal with anybody at the moment.

He wondered again what the hell had possessed him to bargain with that coven of psychotic witches and warlocks.

His fists shook in anger.

Oh yeah. How could he have forgotten? Daddy Dearest had taken his own life, leaving the succession of the pack to his oldest son in his will. Unknown to Strider at the time, he'd also left a mountain of debt to some pretty fucking scary people. Just like the human world, the Underworld had its fair share of mafias and evil overlords. People Strider naively thought would forget all about the debts, since his father had racked them up in his many business ventures, and said father was now very dead.

Strider realized quickly that the idea of them saying "it's all good" was just plain stupid.

The mafia didn't take kindly to being ripped off. Neither did the drug lords. And one day not so long ago, they came to collect.

The result had left him bloodied on the steps of the mansion where his pack lived, with a promise that if he didn't pay up, and fast, they'd come back and kill his pack—while making him watch. He'd been given an impossible deadline to break even, and it was fast approaching.

His eyes felt scratchy, not from crying like a pussy, though he'd definitely shed some tears when they'd broken nearly every bone in his body and left him on his own porch to bleed out. No, his eyes hurt from lack of sleep. He couldn't remember the last time he'd gotten a good night's sleep. Three to four hours were stolen a night, at most. It was hard to find peace enough to relax and drift off when the thought of those assholes coming in and killing everyone you loved loomed over you.

Or he'd think back to his childhood, piecing together the puzzle of his father's rapidly acquired wealth one memory at a time. Now, all the money to pay for expensive vacations and luxurious furnishings while he and his brothers were growing up made sense. "I want you boys to have what I never did," his father, Jake, had often said. "We never had a damn penny while I was growing up. Made life very hard." He said this all the time, to the point of sounding like he worshiped at the Altar of the Dollar.

Some people became addicted to booze or drugs or shopping. Jake Walcutt had been addicted to money.

His father had long been Alpha of the Sherwood Forest Pack. His father really shouldn't have been in charge of anything. But he was the oldest, with most of the other pack members who drifted in and out of their little club being fifteen to twenty years younger than Jake's forty-two years. He'd declared himself the leader one day, when they had all of three members, and the others didn't seem to much give a damn one way or another.

But in the beginning they weren't a large pack, carrying no more than twenty wolves or so at a time. A lot of wanderers or rejects from other walks of life had found a home with them. And when you didn't have a dime to your name, "home" conveniently became wherever you wanted it to be. They never slept among humans. One of their wolves had a habit of Shifting in his sleep. A big wolf with a habit of eating people wasn't good for anyone's safety.

They slept on the bare ground, on a mattress of earth and grass, or if it was wintertime, in tents they'd stolen off of campsites. They were never in one place long enough for the pack members to find steady work.

One day, while they were outside of Chicago, Jake had met a shadowy man inside a bar. Both Strider and his two younger brothers had been dragged inside while "Daddy talked business." Strider remembered sitting at the bar, watching his four-year-old brother, Mike, play with beer-soaked coasters at the bar, while he tried to keep one-year-old Alec, who sat on his lap, from fussing too much. When their dad had emerged from the back with a tall, well-dressed man, he'd had a smug smile on his face. "Just you wait, boys," he hooted as he rejoined them. "We're going to become filthy rich. This is our big break. I'm going to take care of this pack."

He'd been saying the same thing over and over for the past eight years they'd roamed the country, begging for or outright stealing what they needed to survive. Surviving—that was what life was all about. Another of his father's many sayings. But in about another year—the year Strider turned nine—everything changed.

Strider had been out foraging in the woods for plants to eat for dinner when he'd returned to the little glen they'd called home to find his father had found and set up a thirty-foot aboveground swimming pool. "Stole this baby from that fancy pool shop in town," he'd bragged, as if he'd won a trophy. Though the pool was positioned by a river with perfectly good water, he had filled it up with money. And not just Washingtons, but also Grants and Benjamins. More money than Strider had ever seen in his entire life.

When you were nine years old, a swimming pool full of money seemed pretty damn cool. Especially when you could count the times you'd actually held money on one paw. The other pack members thought it was cool, too. No one questioned where it came from, because then it might disappear. No one talked about what had to have been involved to acquire that much money, because if you ignore the problem, it will go away, right?

Within a year, Jake Walcutt had finally made good on his promise. They'd settled in that glen. The aboveground pool had been replaced with an inground one as large as a lake, complete with a fountain and slides. The surrounding forest had been removed, and a mansion worthy of an A-list actor erected. Their father dubbed the surrounding woods "Sherwood Forest" because he thought Robin Hood was cool as shit. Could tell you everything about the man, the myth, the legend. Thus, their pack became known as the Sherwood Forest Pack. More people came as word of the "rich, forest-dwelling pack" spread. Their numbers swelled from twenty members to over a hundred. Even with that many people staying at the mansion, it never seemed crowded. It was hard to fill up twenty thousand square feet.

Expensive cars appeared in their garages, and for the first time in his life, Strider and his brothers didn't have to wear dirty, ripped clothing. Their closets were filled with designer labels. They began to feel secure. And the money kept on coming.

"We deserve all this," Jake said. "Never had anything growing up... the world owes us this."

As Strider would learn when he grew up, the world didn't owe them shit. The world was actually a pretty damn scary place, especially when mobsters were banging down your door, demanding to be reimbursed.

His brothers hadn't helped that situation any. They

grew up spoiled, especially Alec. He'd been too young to remember sleeping on the ground or eating from the forest. The boy had been fed with a silver fucking spoon from the time he was two. And he'd bought into all of Dad's lies. He truly did believe the world owed them this, as payment for making his father suffer for so long.

He blew what money they had whenever and however he could. Mike would go along with it because he didn't have a spine or much of a personality. And because he knew that whatever Alec wanted, Alec got.

Strider hadn't been any help in that department. He should have disciplined Alec more, but to a lesser extent, he too had bought into their father's philosophy about life, money, and that the world owed him riches beyond measure.

What a fool he had been.

Reality had started to sink in when he saw the bank statements and IRS audits after his father's funeral. Jake Walcutt was barely a day into the cold earth when the accountants and bankers came calling.

Not used to dealing with things like "debt" or "foreclosure," he'd buried his head in the sand. His father had believed if you "ignored a problem long enough, it would just go away."

Then the mob came, and shit hit the fan.

Strider sat on the sofa, feeling as if his body were made of stone, and stared at the brand on his wrist. He could blame his father for him selling his soul to the devil, but he knew that would be denial of responsibility. No one had forced him to accept Melaney's offer when she'd found him in a bar one night, drinking away his worries. No one had forced him to kill his old mate so he may acquire her wealth. That still kept him up at night, the look of betrayal and terror in her eyes during her last moments.

Vomit threatened to come up. He bent over the side of the sofa and dry heaved, but nothing would come. That was right—he hadn't had much of an appetite, except for alcohol, the stronger the better, since being visited by the mob. About the only thing he ate was protein shakes, and only after a strenuous workout. Physical activity always took his mind off things. When he was running or lifting or biking, he didn't have to think. He could forget—about the mob, about his spoiled brothers' futures, about the pack who depended on him. All of it.

His foot began to tap.

Taptaptaptaptaptap.

His heart thrummed. His next breath choked him, his throat was so dry and tight.

In another week, the mob would come to collect. Either the money owed them, or the lives of his pack, they said it didn't matter which. A debt could be paid in cash or blood, according to them.

To keep the funds away from his brothers, he'd opened up two private accounts about a year ago. One was a mutual fund wrapped up in an IRA and the other a high-interest savings account. For the IRA he'd gone out on a limb and invested a third of the pack's savings, hoping to earn more than he'd put in and more quickly make up the difference with what was owed. That plan had done fairly well, but not as well as he had hoped. The money would have to sit in there for far longer than he could afford to wait in order to generate enough profit to fully cover the debts. Thus, he'd resorted to plan B—stealing what was owed.

One of their recently joined pack members was adept with hacking. Had made a living stealing tiny fractions of income from high-volume business accounts, where the auditing was too muddied and dense that by the time they caught the theft—if they ever did—he'd have disappeared. Strider had bribed him to do the same for the pack. It had helped, but again, he still had a long way to go to get what he owed the mafia.

Enter Plan C—Operation Bluebeard.

When he was a boy, he never dreamed he'd kill his spouses to collect on inheritance. Or kill other Alphas to obtain their pack's wealth. One of the perks of that had also been more power, since he now controlled well over five hundred werewolves. Obtaining the Whiteclaw Pack, one of the wealthiest packs around, would make up for what was owed.

Some of the members of his pack had jobs. He'd thought about taxing them eighty percent in exchange for pack protection, but he knew he'd quickly lose members with that law. Getting the Whiteclaw Pack, one of the wealthiest in the nation, was his only option this late in the game.

He would obtain that pack at any cost. With Breanna Whiteclaw's reputation for being a hard-ass, he'd suspected he wouldn't be able to as easily woo her as he had the other Alpha female. Ruining her pack's trust in her, ostracizing her from her allies, was the better route. Melaney had been more than happy to assist. The idea of making it seem as if it were a rogue witch attacking the Whiteclaw Pack had been her idea. She'd given him everything he'd needed—the power to destroy, charms to mask his scent and make his werewolf signature appear like that of a witch's, even a charm for invisibility, which he really appreciated. Too bad they all had an expiration date. Melaney had thought it fitting it coincide with the mafia's chosen deadline for him. The eventual loss of the invisibility charm was a pity; he could think of a few uses for it, such as slipping in and out of a bank vault unnoticed. Too bad the charms only worked during the timeframe designated by the witch who created it, down to the exact date and time.

Oh well. He had bigger worries, like making sure his entire pack—all five hundred wolves—wasn't destroyed come one week from today.

Breanna Whiteclaw had to die. That was the only way he could be certain she wouldn't interfere when he became Alpha and started accessing the Whiteclaw Pack's wealth. Before the end of the summit, he guaranteed her pack would mutiny against her—and demand a new Alpha. Then he would challenge her to a fight to the death for the right to her pack.

With renewed resolve, he stood and strode from the room to find his prey.

CHAPTER TEN

THE THING ABOUT BEING SCARY AS HELL WITH A REP TO match is that you can glean information quickly. An advantage, in Shadow's book.

After the chaos had died down and the DPI was done interviewing them, Jack, Breanna, and Shadow split up to track down leads on Strider's true motives. The theory was that most of these old blue bloods with deep networks would be too rattled by all the excitement to notice the snooping.

After another visit to Gramps—aka Captain Scumbag—Shadow had some much-needed direction. The snake had tried rationalizing that this information was the favor he'd promised Shadow earlier.

Shadow had rationalized, on pain of breaking Gramps's face, that it was indeed not.

Gramps had agreed.

He'd started spewing up information once Shadow got

the "I'm going to kill you if you don't start talking" glint to his eyes. The man Shadow was now looking for was Orion Masters, King of the New York City pack, one of the largest and wealthiest packs in the nation. Orion was also one of Strider's former packmates when he was a boy.

The man wasn't hard to track down. Just follow the trail of expensive cigar smoke and extravagant wine. He was in a drawing room with several other Alphas, their mates nowhere to be seen, drinking and smoking and talking business as though the shooting had never happened.

A true gentlemen's party. But Shadow knew from stories of their dirty politics that they were anything but gentlemen.

Shadow paused in the doorway and took a step forward. A hand shot out—apparently the bouncer thought he could stop him. "Alphas only."

Shadow didn't say a word. He soundlessly gripped the man's hand, broke it in several spots with a well-placed squeeze, and kept walking. The bouncer didn't follow, content to stand buckled over in the hallway yowling and swearing.

The men barely looked up. They were probably too distracted by making seven-figure business deals under the radar.

Shadow waltzed right up to a tall, lean man with a charming smile and too much product in his auburn hair. The glossy surface of his finely tailored suit was impeccable, the rose in his pocket as deep a shade of red as his hair.

Orion's gaze flicked up first, doing a double take on Shadow. He paled. One by one the men looked up, and the conversation died down.

"Can I help you?" Orion said with a stiff smile.

"Yeah. I need to talk to you."

"Come back later. I'm in the middle of—"

"That wasn't a request. Now. In private." He walked off. Orion had recognized him. Shadow had seen the awe and fear flash through his eyes upon seeing him. Not to mention the "going white as a ghost" part. He would follow. He knew better than not to.

Sure enough, a few minutes later Orion joined him in the hallway. "Let's walk while we talk," Shadow said, heading off down the hallway, away from the main part of the house where most of the guests were gathered.

Orion didn't look happy about following him, but he complied. Two of his bodyguards slipped in behind him.

Shadow stopped. "Tell them to fall back twenty feet."

Orion stared.

Shadow raised an eyebrow.

Gulping, Orion adjusted the collar on his shirt and glanced at his bodyguards. He must have delivered the message telepathically; without him saying a word they stepped away, glowering at Shadow.

He continued walking at a leisurely pace, Orion alongside him, about two feet away. "Tell me what you know about Strider," Shadow began.

"… He was my packmate."

"I know that. What else?"

"He had it rough growing up."

Shadow turned a flinty gaze at him. "Define rough."

"Living outside, stealing food, spending winters nearly

112

freezing to death because they couldn't afford heat if they did manage to rent a place."

Ah. Shadow was familiar with those types of living conditions. "Go on."

"His father liked to gamble with shady business deals. Said it was the only way to live the American dream anymore and make any real money. He was obsessed with it."

Another familiar vice. Shadow had battled that addiction long ago, when he'd joined the Black Moon Pack and had started earning real dough. He'd never seen that much money in his life. Neither had his parents. Holding onto his newfound wealth and obtaining more by any means necessary had become obsessions.

"One day, he landed a deal that scored him millions," Orion said. "The rest is history."

"What kind of deal?"

"The kind that sends people to jail for life, if not to the electric chair or lethal injection chamber."

Not surprising. With that kind of payout, the price to pay had to be just as steep. "So Strider kept the money?"

Orion stiffened.

Bingo. "What happened?"

Orion's lips pressed together. He glanced at his guards, over his shoulder.

Shadow stopped, tensed. "I hope you're not thinking of ambushing me. It's just a simple question. No reason to get evasive." He cocked his head, studying the Alpha. "Unless you're trying to hide something—or protect someone."

"Something tells me no matter what I do, I won't

be able to protect him from you," Orion said, laughing bitterly.

Damn straight. Shadow waited.

Orion stood there, mouth sealed shut.

Fine. They could do this the hard way. Shadow swung out.

POW!

Orion fell back into the wall, clutching his jaw. "Fuck! You just hit an Alpha, you insubordinate—"

"Actually, I Marked Breanna Whiteclaw earlier. Guess that makes me the same rank as you—an Alpha." The guards rushed forward, weapons drawn, as Shadow grabbed fistfuls of Orion's shirt.

Orion threw up a hand, and the guards halted. "At ease! Don't shoot!"

"Yeah," Shadow drawled, low and icy. "It'd be a shame if I had to use your Alpha as a shield."

That got them to back off.

Orion's face paled. "What do you want?"

"Strider's threatened my woman," Shadow said, eyes narrowing. "As a concerned mate, I have a right to know why." He didn't need to know they weren't technically mated yet.

"I"—another hard swallow—"don't know anything."

"Bullshit. I know you're lying. I can smell your fear."

"Please. I don't—"

Shadow growled, slamming Orion's head against the wall. "Then you're not as useful to me as I thought. And I don't like wasting my time. You're going to tell me you grew up with this prick, and all you know about him is his backstory? Some shit I already knew?" Granted, he hadn't known Strider's history, but again, Orion didn't need to know that. "I expect better intel next time."

"Next time?"

Shadow didn't say another word. Let the guy freak out, unravel a bit. It would make him sloppy.

Maybe he was telling the truth. Maybe he didn't actually know what Strider's motives were. But to save his own ass, he would run to Strider and demand to know what the hell was going on. And with the bug Shadow had just planted on him, he'd learn everything he needed to know.

Orion scrambled away, as if he couldn't run fast enough.

"Remember," Shadow called, "you can run, but you can't hide. Not from me."

That got him going faster.

But not his bodyguards. They stayed. And as soon as their Alpha was safely past them, they charged.

Shadow sighed. "So not in the mood for this right now."

The first guy came at him hard and fast. Shadow barely had time to block the first punch before the next one came. He raised a brow. Impressive. Made even more so by the fact that they both looked as if they'd walked out of a swanky men's cologne ad. "Someone's... taught you... how to fight," he said between grunts and blocks.

Model Number One grunted and kept trying to rearrange Shadow's face. The thrill of the fight flared inside Shadow as he and the guy danced around. He was so busy trying to keep up with the first bodyguard's pace that he'd almost forgotten about the other one. He politely reminded Shadow of his presence by kicking him squarely in the spine.

Shadow felt a pop as he staggered forward, biting back a curse. With his spine screaming in agony, he whirled to attack the other guy, but Bodyguard Number One had other plans. He assaulted him first, going back at it with the punching routine. Meanwhile, the second guy snuck up on Shadow's left.

Ah, he got it. The first guy was meant as a distraction so the second guy could attack. Nice. The two of them had obviously been fighting as a team for a long time.

Shadow, came Breanna's voice inside his head. *Where are you?*

They'd tested out the telepathic bond earlier after their little powwow. It worked, of course, seeing as he was technically part of her pack now by Marking her. A fact none of them, Jack included, still seemed too thrilled about.

I'm a little busy, Shadow said, blocking an uppercut from Guy Number One and narrowly ducking the second guy's massive fist. It went clean through the wall. He grunted—he was stuck.

There was Shadow's chance. Time to end this.

He distantly heard Breanna say something about coming to find him, but he was too focused on taking out Guy Number One while his buddy was preoccupied.

Whirling with lightning speed, he swiftly repaid the guy for all the hurt he'd delivered him with a few swift strikes to the gut and then his temple. The guy crumpled to the ground, unconscious. Shadow smiled at the red welt swelling on the guy's face. That would make an impressive bruise.

Douche bag.

"Asshole!"

The second guy charged with a roar. Shadow braced himself for impact, when Breanna, still wearing that stunning dress, shoved him out of the way and kneed the bodyguard in the stomach. Well, it wasn't so much that she'd kneed him as much as she'd used his own momentum against him. He'd been coming on so fast that he hadn't been able to stop once she'd shoved Shadow out of harm's way.

What happened next dropped his jaw.

Breanna could fight. *Holy hell*, could she fight.

Forget fast—the woman was lethal, a wraith as she zipped around the guy's punches and kicks so quickly, it looked as if he were standing still. She miscalculated a counterattack, not being quick enough to block it. The guy clipped her in the shoulder, meaning to hit her chest, but she'd sidestepped at the last second. Still, the sound of her grunting in pain made Shadow's anger nearly boil over.

He was going to rip this guy's dick off.

Starting forward, Breanna yelled, "I got this!"

The next instant she'd sprung up, wrapped those long legs around the guy's head, and leaned forward. He toppled into the wall, slamming his skull into it, and fell to the ground. She kept her legs squeezing around his throat until his face turned red, then blue, until he at last lost consciousness.

Breathing hard, she finally let go and got up, refusing

Shadow's hand. Her lovely dress had torn, nearly exposing her right breast. Shadow couldn't say he minded.

He stood by quietly, trying to process what had happened. And control his raging libido. God, it was hot when a woman knew how to kick ass. And she'd been doing it to defend him.

Chest still heaving, she at last looked at him. "What?"

Her mouth dropping open, sucking in deep breaths and looking perfectly kissable for it, was too much. He needed her—now.

"Dammit, you're so hot in the heat of battle," he growled, stalking forward with every intention of kissing her dizzy.

He'd gripped a handful of her disheveled hair, tipped her head back, and was about to crush his mouth to hers, when fear flashed in her eyes.

He faltered.

"Stop," she whispered.

He instantly halted. The velvet of her dark voice held more power over him than anyone or anything else had in a long time. Actually, make that ever. It unnerved him.

Taking a few deep breaths, she composed herself, took his hand from her hair, and clasped it. "Come with me. We should talk."

"Agreed," he said. "But before we do that…"

CHAPTER ELEVEN

BREANNA'S MIND WAS STILL REELING WITH JOY AS SHE tugged Shadow outside and into the gardens. A bug. He'd planted a freaking bug on Orion. Brilliant. His ingenuity and quick thinking substantially improved his favor with her.

After telling Jack about the bug and leaving him with her laptop and headphones on "Orion watch" or, as he'd dubbed it, "Operation Catch-an-Asshole," Breanna had commandeered Shadow and headed to the gardens. It seemed like the most logical place to talk privately, considering most of the crowd was still inside, being interrogated by the DPI. Several blue bloods had left, scared off by the gunfire. Breanna couldn't blame them, but she viewed their fleeing with a certain amount of disgust. Alphas were supposed to be unshakable, a strong presence no matter what so their packs may know they could rely on them.

Soft-spined cowards.

Shadow crossed his arms after she'd dragged him a fair distance away from the house. "What exactly did you want to talk about?"

She shifted her weight, looked around. The alcove was covered in climbing red roses. Their velvet petals shimmied in the light autumn breeze, their blossoms full and swollen with perfume. It really was a lovely spot. Plus, it provided a much-needed distraction when her mind went blank and her tongue dry. "Everything, I guess," she finally said. Her throat was raspy. She wanted to blame the earlier fight, but the tickle of nerves in her belly said she couldn't.

God, why was she nervous? Being nervous implied she actually cared about what he thought. Which she shouldn't.

He raised a brow, smiled a little. "Pretty broad topic."

She sighed and went to run her hands through her hair, to comb it out with her fingers. They snagged in the parts that had been pinned back. "Damn these bobby pins to hell!" She began yanking them out and casting them on the ground. Not that there were many. She'd made her hairdresser swear to use but a handful, on pain of death, because anything that caused pain to her scalp was created by the devil and worthy of death. Especially when her head already hurt enough as it was.

The bodyguard had been good—very good, she admitted. She prided herself on being fast and agile, but she hadn't quite been fast enough. He'd walloped her once on her head, and her shoulder. An unattractive, if not impressive, bruise was forming there. Which was fine. She'd never been one to get worked up over a few scrapes and bruises. Her father had her combat instructors beat her ass more severely if she so much as sniffled when she got hit in the ring. "Crying doesn't accomplish anything," Bear Whiteclaw had said. A saying she agreed with, for the most part. But crying sure as hell was useful for purging yourself of all the unwanted, heavy emotional baggage you didn't want.

Shadow watched her sigh in contentment once her head was bobby-pin-free. She ran her hands through her hair to tame it. She didn't much give a damn what it looked like at the moment, a sentiment that was growing stronger by the second. What she'd really like was a hot bath, preferably with Shadow.

Her cheeks heated. The heat seemed to drip down to her loins, making them ache. She cleared her throat and turned away. Fucking hell, now she was reduced to being a miserable, lust-struck pup. Since when had impure thoughts ever made her blush?

Grow up.

She leaned against a hedgerow, massaging her scalp. God, it felt good to be rid of those dreadful bobby pins. Though right now she didn't mind the ache in her scalp. It was a welcome distraction from the tingling of her sex as Shadow approached. He leaned on the hedgerow next to her, turning his back to it as she had and resting the back of his head against it. The air heated between their bodies, and the aroma of pine and snow surrounded her.

Curiously, she sniffed, wanting more of it. Earlier, she would have done anything to be rid of the smell—and him—completely.

What a difference a few hours and a life-or-death situation could make, she thought wryly.

She at last dropped her hands. He was waiting for her to speak, and she knew good and well she was stalling. Don't be a pussy—that was another of her father's rules. "Bear never wanted children—he wanted weapons, heirs, pawns. My mother…" Her throat closed up, as it always did when speaking of her mom. "My mother was always in frail health. She had some kind of condition that left her with a weak immune system. Being of old blood like my father, her parents married her off to Bear via arranged marriage when she was eighteen. She bore many babies for him over the years, none of which survived except me. I almost didn't make it either, being born five weeks premature, with several health complications. But my father was confident I would live. He said I was a survivor, just like him." She smiled wistfully, then her voice grew quiet. Part of her didn't even know entirely why she was telling Shadow all this, but she felt the compulsion to continue.

"Mom passed away. Dad never remarried. Said he had other things to worry about other than a fussy, frail wife. Bear always did view women as the weaker sex," she said, the words bitter and brittle in her mouth. "Determined to mold me into the son he'd been robbed of, he began training me in the arts of fighting and death as soon as I could throw a punch." She stared out into the garden, which blurred into the distant past. "I was never allowed to go to dances, never allowed to hang out with friends. He wanted to be the center of my world. He needed me to need him so he could ensure I was completely dependent on him and would never wish to run away. Because if I ever managed to, he would lose his heir—another pawn." She smirked. "Didn't stop me from dreaming of it. Though I guess, in a way, he got his wish. Despite my resentment and anger toward him for robbing me of a normal childhood and depriving me of unconditional love, he was my father. The only family I've ever known, not including my packmates. And because of that, I miss him by default, I suppose."

"I'm sorry," Shadow said quietly after a thoughtful silence.

"Don't be." She shrugged. "Not your fault. And it's in the past." Her voice sounded more ragged than she wanted it to be. Shifting her weight away from him, she crossed her arms and looked away. Her irritation grew alongside the silence. Honestly, what had she been expecting? For him to spill his heart just because she had?

Angry with herself, she was about to mutter, "Forget it," when his whisper made her freeze.

"I murdered my entire team."

She couldn't have heard him right. More tense silence ensued. It felt like an eternity before he continued.

"My... previous employer—not Drake, the one before him, and not counting all the shitty odd jobs I held just to make ends meet—but—"

"The one where you killed people."

"Yes, to put it bluntly." He took a breath, let it out, scratched his head. His eyes kept darting to and from her face, as if he couldn't bear to meet her gaze head-on. "On my last night with that organization, my crew and I were on a mission. Our goal was to capture and kill a group of vampires who'd been gruesomely murdering children throughout the country."

"Jesus."

"Well, we caught 'em, but our intel had left out some crucial details. Like how one of them was telepathic and another was a necromancer. Oh, and they were both children themselves, with grudges against their childhood bullies. Because of said grudges, they insisted on carrying out revenge on any child they could find."

She stared at him. Dear God.

"They raised an army of the dead, killed my whole pack within minutes. Thing is, I could have stopped it before it started, if I'd killed the girl. The Master. But I didn't. I froze. I… she, the little girl…" He shook his head.

"What?" she asked gently.

His voice warbled and broke. "She reminded me too much of my little sister, Amelia."

"Amelia?"

"She's dead. Killed herself. I could have stopped it. She'd been talking about it for a long time, but she was always so dramatic. I thought she was joking, even though I knew she was depressed. Never did I believe…"

She rested a hand on his arm, her heart heavy with sympathy for him. "I'm sorry."

He took a deep breath and let it out in a rush, blinking his glistening eyes. He cracked a smile. It was one of those zany ones people get when they're either upset or nervous. "Anyway, I left the bounty-hunting business for good after my pack died. One, because I was pissed at my employer for fucking up the intel. They apologized a million times, made it out like it was some mistake. But I heard about the life-insurance benefits they collected off my crew upon their deaths."

"You think it was staged."

"Yes. I know it was. But I can't prove it. Well, I can, but they're disbanded now anyway. Went bankrupt. The owner had made a few bad investments. Sucked the organization dry of cash and then some. My retribution came when I saw them foreclosing on the CEO's house and hauling away everything but the clothes on his back. They did take his watch. He rather fancied it. I'll never forget the look on his face as he sat on the steps of a home he used to own, watching everything he'd worked for literally vanish, when the executor came over and said there was a watch missing from the estate's inventory. He demanded it on the spot."

Jesus. "What happened to the vampires?"

"They fled overseas, tried to go underground, but by then word had spread in Europe about what they'd done. Someone else took them out in France. Turns out the French hate child-killers, too."

She stood there, stunned. Holy fuck. Intense grief, unlike anything she'd ever felt before, not even when her father had died, poured off of Shadow and into her through their growing bond. Had she known all this from the start, of the guilty burden he carried, would she have treated him any differently?

Not knowing what else to do, she took his hand and held it. Not squeezing, just holding it. Letting him know he wasn't alone in this.

He looked at her, really looked at her, and gave her a soft smile. His eyes seemed lighter, having relieved himself of the secrets in his chest.

She slowly smiled back.

Breanna, came Jack's voice so abruptly in her head that it startled her.

You don't have to yell, she snapped. *What is it? Did Orion make a move?*

I don't know. Maybe.

What do you mean 'maybe'?

I mean, I just heard from Bailey back at home. There's been another attack.

CHAPTER TWELVE

Shadow and Breanna were on a plane by dawn, heading back to her home in upstate Virginia. It had been relatively easy to get permission from the High King to leave the summit. For one, he was distracted as all get-out by the ailing queen and preparing for another possible attack. Breanna also pulled the "my pack was just under attack and according to law blah blah blah, the Alpha has the right to return home" card. The only catch was Jack had to stay behind as her pack's representative. He promised to alert them to any news, whether that be about the attacks at the summit or if Orion met with Strider. So far he hadn't, but Shadow was confident he'd break sooner or later and request a meeting with his childhood pal.

"They always break," Shadow had said.

"Who?" Breanna had asked.

"The weak-willed ones."

The temperature was noticeably colder in Marion,

Virginia, which Breanna was well prepared for. Shadow... not so much.

"It's fucking freezing," he said as they got into the fire-engine-red Honda Accord Breanna and Jack had left parked at the airport. Breanna drove, while Shadow rode shotgun.

"Get used to it, precious," Breanna said, flashing Shadow a grin before gunning it out of the garage.

She drove like a stunt driver. *Damn, I thought my driving was ludicrous,* Shadow thought as she wove in and out of traffic, honking the horn when two slower-moving vehicles boxed them in.

Breanna swore, drumming the nails of her free hand along her leg. Her other hand clenched the steering wheel so tightly her knuckles turned white.

Shadow finally took her free hand and squeezed. *It will be all right,* he said, testing out the mate-bond forming between them.

She finally looked at him. The worry gathered in her eyes made him want to hold her, stroke her hair, soothe away her fears. "You don't know what it's been like," she said aloud. "The pack... since the attacks, they've grown more distant from me. More distrustful of my ability to lead and protect them like my father did."

"We'll prove them wrong. Together."

She tried smiling, but it looked forced.

Her nerves continued saturating their bond all the way back to Whiteclaw Manor. The house was grand, built with Victorian elegance in mind. Sitting two stories tall, it was a pale-blue house with white trim, a wraparound porch and balcony, roses, roses, and more red roses surrounding the foundation, and a tall black wrought-iron gate surrounding the property. A large garage, painted to match, sat off to one side, as well as a parking lot and a winding paved driveway that looped in front of the house and back out again toward the country highway.

The property was bare, spotless hills of rolling green grass, save for the private lake behind the house. A large inground swimming pool sat near the lake, along with a tennis court and volleyball pit.

Shadow whistled as Breanna pulled to the front of the house and parked. "Damn," he said as they got out. "Bear had good taste in real estate."

"He had expensive taste in real estate," Breanna said with a glower. "It might be pretty to look at, and it sure as hell impresses guests, but property taxes and home owner's insurance are a bitch."

Shadow wouldn't know. He'd never owned his own home. Never really had the desire to be tied down to one place, until now. Until he'd looked at her and known, for better or for worse, their destinies were intertwined.

Breanna marched straight to the house. Shadow followed, thinking it strange no one came out to greet them. There was an undercurrent of tension in the air, like when you walked into a haunted house and sensed you weren't alone. Something—or rather, someone—didn't want them there. They just hadn't shown themselves yet.

He looked around, studying his surroundings, prepping for someone to strike.

Paranoid much? he chided himself, but to hell with it.

He wasn't taking any chances.

The inside of the house was dizzying to look at. Every surface seemed to have some kind of decoration or pattern to it: patterns on the wallpaper, patterns on the upholstery in the furniture, patterns on the curtains, patterns on the ceilings, patterns on the rugs, patterns even carved into the door and window frames. It was almost visually overwhelming. The only words that came to mind were "chaotic" and "busy." Everything was clean, polished to a mirror-like shine. The air smelled of lemon furniture polish; someone had been dusting recently. A trio of candles flickered from a bookshelf overlooking one of many great stone fireplaces in the many great rooms throughout the house.

"You have a lovely home," Shadow said.

"Glad you like it," Breanna murmured absently. She seemed to be looking for someone, flitting room to room so fast Shadow had a hard time keeping up.

At last, they found someone. And Shadow immediately wished they hadn't.

Breanna stopped short in the doorway to what appeared to be a sitting room. Couches and chairs sat in a large circle. And on those couches and chairs sat ten very pissed-off-looking people—werewolves.

And each of them had a gun or knife or some manner of weapon in their hands.

"What's all this?" Breanna asked, looking about. She still hadn't moved from the doorway.

A gangly teenaged girl with freckles and long red hair glanced anxiously at the others before standing. "Welcome home, Breanna," she said, coming to give her a hug.

Breanna hugged her back. "Hello, Bailey. Thank you for calling us. What happened?"

"What happened is our Alpha was off kissing royal ass and sipping on fine wine, leaving the rest of us here to fend for ourselves!" cried a rotund man who appeared to be in his fifties. A few shouts of agreement went up.

Shadow growled, but Breanna clamped down on his arm and discreetly shook her head.

She seemed to steel herself, ignoring the comment. "Where's Jamar?" she asked Bailey. "Is he still in the hospital?"

Bailey shook her head. "No, ma'am. He's here."

Breanna looked relieved. "I'll go see him—"

"He doesn't want to see you."

A tall, beautiful, dark-skinned woman stood, glaring at Breanna with tears in her eyes. She had a proud jut to her chin.

Breanna's eyes softened. "Mrs. Wheaton, I'm terribly sorry for the tragedy that befell your son. Please know I never meant for any of it to happen."

"But it happened," Mrs. Wheaton said. "It happened because of you!"

Murmurs of agreement, the nod of heads. More glares thrown Breanna's way.

"Bear was no benevolent master, but he was a good one," Mrs. Wheaton said, her tawny eyes never breaking Breanna's steadfast gaze. "He kept us safe. There wasn't a doubt in our minds he could protect us. Since Bear died, God rest his soul, and you took over, you've done nothing but bring us pain and suffering."

"That's not true," Breanna said, stepping forward. "I've sacrificed everything to run this pack. If you had any idea—"

"Oh, don't go defending yourself! You're just trying to make yourself feel better for doing a piss-poor job of—"

"That's enough," Shadow snarled. He'd stood back as Breanna had asked, clenching his fists and jaw, but no more. His patience had reached a breaking point. He stepped into the room.

Mrs. Wheaton instantly went silent. Everyone seemed to sink back into their chairs, gazing up at him with a mixture of distrust and fear.

"My name is Shadow."

Someone snorted. Shadow looked at him.

The someone stopped snickering and gulped.

"As I was saying," Shadow said, not without irritation and with the cold calmness that made people sit up and listen, "I am here because I've Marked your Alpha. Therefore, that technically makes me your Alpha."

"Have you mated her yet?" a lanky man with big glasses asked.

"No," Shadow said without hesitation. "Not yet. The reason being we haven't had a chance to mate. I only Marked her recently. Due to the disturbances at the summit and here, we've had too much going on. What's more important is keeping this pack safe, which is exactly what we came back to do. If something happens or you have a problem, you can come to either Breanna or myself. But it better be a legitimate fucking problem and not more whining. Because what I see are a bunch of spoiled, whiny children. Grow up. This is a pack, not a daycare. Starting right now, everyone pitches in with guard duty."

Protests went up. Shadow's snarl silenced it.

"You will help out, to put forth an effort to protect this pack, or so help me I'll start banishing people."

"You—you can't do that!"

"That's not fair!"

"Who the hell do you think you are?"

"I've already told you—I'm your Alpha. It is fair, I can do it, and I will fucking do it if you do not comply. 'Pack before self.' That's something all packs teach. Memorize it. Take it to heart. Those who don't want to can take a hike. In wartime, we don't have room for freeloaders."

He waited for a response. Breanna stared at him, mouth agape, while the rest of the room glared.

"That's what I thought," Shadow said. "You'll be given your assignments in one hour, after my mate and I have had time to discuss the matter further."

Without another word, he turned and strode from the room. Breanna swiftly followed. As soon as they were gone, the wolves started murmuring to one another.

Shadow didn't care. Let them talk. He'd just given them plenty to discuss and mull over. And he'd meant every word.

Though he had no clue where the hell he was going, he kept up his purposeful stride. Breanna at last grabbed him and pulled him into a room. A large mahogany desk sat before a wall filled with bookshelves and filing cabinets. More shelves and office equipment sat about the room, making it feel almost cluttered. The décor was girly, as were the color choices—rose and gold.

She shut and locked the door and sighed hard, leaning against the wall. "This is my office. We won't be disturbed here."

Shadow raised a brow, looking around.

"My decorator picked out the colors, not I," she said with a roll of her eyes.

He smiled a little. Already she was reading his mind.

She crossed her arms, studied him. "While that verbal kick-to-the-balls was needed," she admitted, "did you really have to threaten to banish them?"

"Would Bear have done the same?"

She pursed her lips.

Point for Shadow. "Look, I think the way to get their respect back is to be more like Bear. He might have been a dick—sorry, sorry, stop glaring at me—but he was a no-nonsense kind of Alpha. They need more of the same. A lot of people don't adapt very well to change. I mean, they can adapt to your style, which seems more nurturing, but it will take time. Right now, given the present threats, we need to stand united. We won't survive otherwise."

Breanna nibbled her bottom lip and at last sighed in surrender. "Something tells me you have a plan. What else did you have in mind?"

CHAPTER THIRTEEN

THEY CONVENED IN THE OFFICE FOR A TOTAL OF FIFTEEN minutes before settling on a plan of action. At least it couldn't be said that they screwed around, especially not with Shadow involved. He was a man of action, something Breanna admired because it reminded her so much of her father. Shadow could be gruff like him, too, but not to the point of being cruel. Which she very much appreciated.

The pack members were still arguing when they left, all but Bailey, whom Breanna had telepathically summoned. Bailey had slipped away from the crowd on pretense of having to use the restroom then had met them down the hall. After gleaning from her where Jamar had been attacked, Shadow and Breanna had escaped out the back of the house and into the quiet countryside.

"Jamar was one of your patrolmen?" Shadow asked as they trekked across the spongy grass bordering the lake. It seemed extra thick, considering it had plenty of water to drink.

Breanna nodded. "Jamar grew up on a military base. His dad was in the army. Moved the family around a lot when Jamar was a kid, before he was killed in action overseas. Jamar enlisted too but was bitten by a werewolf on one of his first missions. When he and his mother came to our pack, he instantly signed up for guard duty. I think it made him feel more at home, give him something familiar to do."

Shadow peppered the conversation with more questions regarding her people and the attacks. What she really would like to have done was speak to Jamar about the incident, but Bailey had advised her against it. Open and honest, Bailey was as close to a second adviser as Breanna had. Still being a kid, she saw the world through a different lens. Breanna wished she could go back to that stage of innocence. Honestly, she didn't think she'd ever been truly innocent, not when Bear Whiteclaw was so determined to turn her into a warrior.

Brushing thoughts of her lost childhood aside, she focused on the task at hand. "Bailey said it happened over there, by those lilac bushes."

"You guys are really into flowery shit, aren't you?" Shadow said.

Breanna was about to snap at him, when she caught his smile. "You're teasing."

He grinned. "Yeah. With Bear's reputation I almost expected barbed wire and booby traps."

"Actually, he wanted something like that, to turn this place into a fortress," she said wryly. "But his landscaper talked him out of it. Said he'd get more property value by making the place look pretty. If Bear spoke a second language, it was money."

Shadow grunted.

Breanna reminisced about her father. He really had been money hungry, cherishing it and bloodshed more than he had his daughter. And look where it got him. For a moment, Breanna felt almost grateful Shadow had killed him. Then she felt terrible. Who on earth would think something like that? Who would "be grateful" their own father was dead, and murdered, no less? Who on earth would be considering actually marrying—or in this case, mating—the man who had killed her father? The Underworld was a fucked-up place led by fucked-up people who reveled in even more fucked-up politics. And, clearly, she was no exception to the norm.

They approached the scene of the crime, which looked oddly idyllic and not at all the kind of place where a violent attack would happen. You'd picture something like a dark alley in some city's gangster-land, or a lonely stretch of highway surrounded by darkened woods in the middle of nowhere. Not some place that looked as if it could be the set for a Victorian romance flick.

Shadow and Breanna both slowly walked around, surveying the land with a critical eye. A branch on the lilac bush was broken; that much Breanna had spotted right away. According to Bailey's account, Jamar had crashed into the bush out of dizziness after feeling as though all the air had been sucked out of his lungs. Something invisible had strangled him, to the point he'd passed out, but not before he'd called for help through the pack-bond. His fellow patrolmen rushed to his aid. Luckily, one of the patrolmen is also a warlock. Upon seeing no physical enemy, he'd taken a wild guess and performed a counterspell. Just in time too. If Jamar had gone any longer without air, he might not be alive.

Breanna made a mental note to reward that warlock at the first viable chance.

"Stop!"

Breanna froze, her foot in midair. Shadow knelt and, after snapping on a glove, retrieved something from the ground—a thin, gray hair.

"You're joking," she said, glancing at the pretty gray rocks beneath her foot. They were the landscaper's idea. "How did you see that? It was practically camouflaged."

"Let's just say I've developed a knack for spotting the 'overlookable.'" His tone was noticeably colder, the gray of his eyes turning darker. Shadow examined the hair, eyes narrowed.

Breanna bit her lip. Dammit. She should have known he'd picked it up from his days as a bounty hunter, an occupation he clearly regretted. But now wasn't the time for apologies or sympathies. They had work to do, a pack to save.

An asshole to put down.

"What do you think?" she asked.

"Animal. It's too coarse to have come from a human." He sniffed, grinned. "No smell either. Smart bastard—or bitch, depending on what we're dealing with. They weren't thorough enough to double-check the area to make sure

they hadn't left behind clues giving away their identity—
probably because your pack intervened with the attack
and scared him or her off—but they were magic-savvy
enough to mask their smell." He licked the hair. "Covered
up the taste, too. We're going to need a DNA test."

"Great. That could take weeks, knowing the DPI."

"You don't have any contacts there?"

Breanna winced. "No one my father hasn't pissed off.
I'm still working on rebuilding those alliances and friend-
ships, if I ever get them back."

"Another worry for another day. No matter. I have
someone who can deal with it." He pulled out one of several plastic Ziploc bags they'd brought, and dropped the
hair inside. "We should check the other attack sites while
we're out and about."

"But wouldn't the perpetrator have cleaned up the
area by now?"

"Not necessarily. We did find a hair."

A hair. Something seemingly insignificant, but all she
had to go off of right now. It was a start.

They combed the rest of the area but didn't find any
more clues. Not even a whiff of magic, wolf, or other creature could be smelled in the air. Deciding they should get
back in case the criminal was lurking nearby, they began
walking back toward the house.

The air was heavy with water, and cool. A natural waterfall resided on the property's edge, the river that created
it wrapping around the fence line and winding through
the countryside.

Shadow paused on a rocky ledge, staring at the

tumbling, laughing water with saddened eyes.

Breanna joined him, watching the water rush over and down the cliffside and out and away at a much lazier pace.

"Amelia loved waterfalls," Shadow at last said, still staring. "Loved nature, animals. She was a gentle soul, despite all the violence she'd seen growing up."

Breanna's heart ached. Yearning to comfort him, she reached out and squeezed his hand. "It's not your fault. No matter what you think. For the longest time I blamed myself for my father's death. Then I blamed you because it was easier." She took a deep breath, sighed it out. "Truth is, it was Bear's fault. He'd placed a target on his back the day he decided to become a monster."

Shadow was looking at her now, a question in his eyes.

She pulled him around to face her, raised her hands, and cupped his cheeks. They were warm and red from walking. The warmth seeped down into his skin. She idly caressed her thumbs over his jawline, loving the way his faint stubble scratched them.

"It's not your fault," she said again, stronger. "Just as it isn't mine. We both need to make peace with it. They were responsible for their own lives. Nothing we said or did can change their decisions and the repercussions of them. We need to let them go."

He exhaled a long, sighing breath, a small smile uplifting his mouth. He touched his forehead to hers, and they breathed deeply for a few precious seconds, eyes closed, listening to the sound of one another's breaths.

"Thank you," he rasped at last.

Breanna searched his eyes. Maybe it wasn't a

punishment or some cruel twist of fate that had caused him to Mark her. Maybe he had been sent to her so she could learn to forgive herself, and thus, give him permission to let go of his own guilt.

Maybe they were sent to heal each other.

She was tired of holding on to the pain, the anger, the regret. Tired of living in the past, spending all her energy on guilt, and driving away her personal happiness because she was so determined to hold someone—Shadow—responsible for her father's death. It was Bear's fault. If anyone were responsible for his own death, it was him.

Not her.

Not Shadow.

Not anyone else.

It was time to let it go. Time to move on and focus on the future.

And just like that, her body felt lighter. The last remnants of bitterness and hatred left her, leaving her feeling weary and raw inside, as if those dark emotions had clawed out everything that made her *her*. She shivered. If she'd kept holding on to them, they very well could have destroyed her.

She'd nearly disappeared, all because she couldn't let go and forgive.

I forgive you, Father. I forgive you for not letting me grow up like a normal child, for ignoring me all the time, for showing me cruelty instead of kindness, and for abandoning me when I needed you most. That's all on you. It's no longer going to be my burden to bear.

She let out a shuddering breath—and smiled.

In one of those rare, quiet moments, despite everything that had happened these past few months, the world literally stopped. Nothing else mattered, not the drama, not the pain, not the bullshit.

Shadow leaned in and kissed her.

This time, she closed her eyes and surrendered.

Her body flared to life at his touch as he pulled her closer, slipping those big, warm hands beneath her shirt and pressing them firmly against her bare back.

She moaned as his tongue slipped into her mouth, his kisses growing hotter, more demanding. He backed her up to a rock face, hoisting her up as she wrapped her legs around his waist. The bulge of his crotch grinded against her as his hips began to rock, thrusting with need.

Heat built within her, growing below her navel and making her blood race. Her pert nipples tingled from the friction against his chest. She couldn't help it—she bit his lip, not hard enough to draw blood but hard enough to get his attention.

She wanted to mate—now. Ceremony be damned.

A growl was her answer. He grasped her shirt. She heard fabric tear. Her hands were on their way to fumbling with his belt buckle when her cell went off, startling them both.

They looked at each other, panting hard as the phone belted out a country tune.

Shadow raised a brow. "Garth Brooks?"

Breanna sighed, reaching for her phone. "Jack's ringtone. He's into country, big time." She pressed Talk. "What's up?" she said, a little sharper than she meant to.

"He did it. Orion went to Strider, just like Shadow thought he would."

Breanna's heart stuttered. "You recorded the conversation?"

She could practically see Jack smiling. "You bet your sweet ass I did."

CHAPTER FOURTEEN

THEY HURRIED BACK TO THE HOUSE AS FAST AS THEY could, despite wanting to linger by the waterfall and finish what they'd started. Breanna found the sound file Jack had sent to her personal email, nestled among a pile of junk mail. Ugh. She really needed to be more selective about opting in to online mailing lists. The twenty-five percent off or whatever incentive they offered wasn't worth the gazillion emails they bombarded her with.

Shadow and she were alone in her office, doors locked, blinds drawn. Her resident warlock had soundproofed the room long ago from physical or magical eavesdroppers, but that still didn't mean she shouldn't be careful. Shutting off the audio on the computer speakers, she offered Shadow the other earbud, its mate already tucked into her ear. He accepted and donned it, and she hit play in the media center.

In the recording, a door closed, and hurried, heavy

footsteps plodded across the wooden floor. "He knows," said a worried voice.

Orion, Shadow said to Breanna through their mate-bond.

There was a swirl of ice in a glass. "Knows what?" came Strider's arrogant, bored voice.

"Shadow!" Orion hissed, lowering his voice as if afraid to speak his name.

Beside her, Shadow smirked.

She rolled her eyes, as if to say, "Yeah, yeah, I know you're happy about scaring the shit out of people. Now get over yourself."

"What do you mean 'he knows'?" Strider asked, though an edge had sharpened his tone like a knife. "Knows what? You'd better quit being so cryptic. I don't do well with being dragged out of important meetings for nonsense."

"I told you it was urgent! But you wouldn't listen!" Orion snapped, sounding agitated and more than a little nervous. "You insisted on dragging your feet, that what I had to say was not important. And now you may very well be screwed because you delayed meeting with me."

There was a growl and the sound of something tipping over—a chair?—as footsteps rushed across the room, and something or someone slammed into a wall with a thud. "Don't scold me like I'm your pup. Out with it."

"Shadow found me. He was fishing for information about you. Trying to figure out why you want the Whiteclaw Pack so badly."

"Was he now?" Strider mused. "That's no concern of mine."

It's about to be, Shadow growled.

Breanna shushed him with a finger pressed firmly to her mouth and a pointed look thrown in his direction.

It sounded as if Strider was walking away, evidently dismissing the conversation.

"You should be worried," Orion said, his voice raspy, as if Strider had tried to strangle him. "Do you have any idea who that man is? What he's done, what he's capable of?"

"Of course I am! I'm not a fool. I've done my research. And I tell you, I'm not afraid of him. I always get what I want no matter who stands in my way. Mark my words: The Whiteclaw Pack will be mine by the end of the month."

"Breanna will never mate you."

"Who said anything about mating?"

Her throat constricted. So he was thinking of killing her or having her unseated from her position via mutiny or a challenge.

Bring it on.

She was a Whiteclaw, and she would bow to no one.

Orion kept talking. "So you're going to dispose of her?"

"By any means necessary."

"But… but that's—"

"Some have what it takes to rule, while others can only follow." There were footsteps, then the sound of a door creaking open. "If all you can do is cower in the face of your enemies, then perhaps you should reconsider your right to be an Alpha."

"How—how dare you!"

"How dare you! If you're going to call yourself a King of Wolves, then you damn well better make sure you have the right to be one. Man up and get out. I have work to attend to. Don't bother me again unless you have something truly worthwhile to say."

Orion was silent. "You know, I remember a boy from years ago who was a hell of a lot better person than the man who stands before me today. You've let wealth and power warp your mind and spirit. I pity you. But I will not help you anymore."

"I don't recall asking for your help."

"Good-bye, Strider."

The door slammed shut a moment later, and the recording ended.

Shadow took his earbud out and crossed his arms. *What do you think?* he asked her telepathically.

She chewed on her lip. *I don't know. I thought he might try to dethrone me. I didn't know that might mean murder.*

We should report this.

To whom? The DPI? He has them in his pocket. Besides, we don't know anything other than the fact that he's going to try to get rid of me, and that we already knew. It's a threat, but they can't hold him on threats. And without being able to prove it's their voices on the recording, we're kind of screwed. Besides, isn't the wire you placed on Orion kind of illegal?

Maybe. But that's beside the point.

She growled in frustration. *I'm so sick of this. Sometimes I wish I could just—* She froze, her mind brewing up ideas faster than she could process them. *Oh, sweet Jesus, this is insane.*

What? Shadow said, watching her. *You've thought of something. Out with it.*

She licked her lips. *This is going to sound crazy...*

CHAPTER FIFTEEN

C

THE PLAN WAS LUDICROUS. "SUICIDAL" HAD BEEN Shadow's word for it. But for Breanna, it may very well be her only chance at getting rid of Strider for good.

She paced the length of her bedroom, gnawing at the fingernails she'd lacquered in hot-pink polish only an hour ago. She smirked. Her childhood etiquette teacher would have had a fit over her chewed-up nails. As always when she thought of her younger years, a wave of resentment and bitterness washed up with those memories. Yesterday, before she'd had her epiphany by the waterfall, she would have let those feelings take over, let them build upon all the dark thoughts she'd collected and harbored over the long years.

Today, she refused to let them change her, to give the seed of hatred and vengeance any more room to grow. She'd buried that monster yesterday, laid those old ghosts to rest in the woods. She and Shadow both.

They'd spent last night apart, thinking and prepping and healing. Sometimes stark quiet and solitary reflection were necessary to piece the soul and the heart back together.

She'd cried. A lot. Far more tears had come out of her than she thought she'd had left after those first initial days upon realizing her father was gone and was never coming back. Even then, some of those tears had been tears of relief, which only made her cry more out of shame. Sometimes she really despised Bear Whiteclaw for the man, the monster, he'd been. Sometimes she was glad to be rid of him. And sometimes, deep in her heart, she missed him terribly. And all of that was okay.

A knock sounded at the door. A moment later, Shadow entered.

Breanna kept up her relentless pacing. "Don't start with me. I'm still going through with it."

"I know you are. I'm not here to stop you." His voice was soft, his eyes scratchy. As though he'd been up all night.

Breanna had a feeling he'd been dealing with some pretty heavy shit last night, too. She'd spent half the night crying or screaming into her pillow, letting go of all that negative energy she'd built up. And there had been a lot. Today, despite the worry that Strider could very well kill her if he found out what she was up to, the rest of her body felt a ton lighter. She'd needed the purge, to release all her anger—they both had.

Shadow sat down on her bed and stared at his hands on his lap. "You're brave. And a good Alpha. If your pack knew what you were willing to do for them, the lengths you'd go to protect them…" He shook his head. "It's a shame they treat you the way they do. They don't deserve you as their leader. And don't you dare ever let them make you feel worthless, you hear?"

Breanna crossed the room to sit beside him. She rested her head on his shoulder. His presence anchored her in the moment, a quiet, solid strength she knew in her heart of hearts she could rely on anytime, anyplace. "Thank you. But I don't do this because I'm seeking someone's approval or because I feel obligated to protect them. I'm an Alpha because it's who and what I am. I don't know how to be anything else. And when I'm not doing a good job, I don't feel like myself."

"I know the feeling. I used to think killing and lying and thieving were all I was good for. I didn't know how to fit into another role, a more 'natural' role in the world. Probably why I fumbled from dead-end job to dead-end job for as long as I did before eventually returning to a similar line of work." He grinned, but it was sour. "Guess I was born to be a killer."

"No," she murmured, raising her head to look at him. "You're a hero. I… had Bailey track down information on your background. Hacking, and anything techie, in general, are hobbies of hers."

Shadow tensed.

She smiled warmly, gazing at him with admiration and understanding and something that might very well grow into love someday. "I know why you did it, now. Why you were a bounty hunter. It wasn't for the bounty or for the thrill of the hunt. You took down criminals because you wanted to keep people safe, to keep your friends and loved ones safe. Some of the people you faced, the things they'd done…" She shivered, her stomach turning at even thinking about them. "Facing them, despite the odds stacked against you, took true courage and selflessness. At first I thought you were a glory seeker, that you were doing it on some selfish whim. But I know better now." She fluttered her fingers over the tattoos covering his arms. "Instead of marking yourself out of penance, I think you should start looking at these as reminders of all the good you've done in the world. For you have done well, Shadow." Her eyes twinkled as she cocked her head to the side. "Or should I say Marcus Stone."

His breath caught, his eyes widening a fraction. His hands began to shake. "Do you have any idea how long it's been since someone's called me by my true name?" He blinked and shook his head with a laugh, his whole face lighting up. "Bailey's a lot better at digging up information than you let on. I think my father was the last person to call me that."

Breanna touched his face. "What do you want me to call you?"

His eyes searched hers as he thought about it. "Marcus. I think it's time I went back to being who I truly was."

She nodded and leaned in with a sly, sexy grin. Her lips hovered over his. "Just for the record, I thought Shadow was wicked-hot."

He chuckled. "Is that so? You know what else is wicked-hot? You in that sheer, low-cut white blouse, black bra, and pencil skirt."

A thrill fluttered through her as he rubbed his palm up and down the skin-hugging, leathery material of her skirt. "Then I'll bet you love the matching panties and garters I have on."

He went rigid. At first, she thought with smug satisfaction that it was because of how turned-on he was. Then she felt it, too, the familiar crackling paranormal signature of another werewolf at their door.

Strider had arrived.

They reluctantly parted, the nervous tension in the room shooting up a couple of degrees. "Sure I can't convince you to change into something more conservative and save the sexy for me later?" Shadow asked as he walked her to the bedroom door. His eyes held a faint golden sheen. Already he considered her his alone. It stoked her lust and made her heart beat wildly.

"You know as well as I do that it will distract him. And we need him off his guard, if we're to get him to confess to the attacks and, I'm certain, an assortment of other crimes," she said, all business. Though the thought of Strider's slimy eyes roving over her body, undressing her in his mind, made her skin shrivel up.

"Yeah, I know," Shadow grumbled, scowling. "Doesn't mean I like it."

"I don't either. But we need every advantage we can get if we're to pull this off."

He gripped her shoulders, keeping her from leaving. "Be careful, all right? Summon me if at any time you feel too uncomfortable. I'll be watching and listening."

"I know." She leaned forward and kissed him. "I'll call if something happens. Trust me to handle this, okay? Bear trained me well."

"I have no doubt he did," Shadow murmured, worry still collected in his eyes.

They parted ways, him squeezing her hand before finally letting go. Squaring her shoulders and lifting her chin high, she marched downstairs and into the parlor, where she'd instructed the doorman to park Strider.

He looked up as she entered, his eyes widening slightly and immediately sweeping her whole body.

That didn't take long, she thought with disgust.

A lusty smile spread across his face. "Leather looks good on you. So does the lace."

She smiled back, having to put real effort into loosening it up enough to appear genuine. "Glad to hear it. Please, sit. We have important business to discuss."

He raised his brows, taking a seat across from her. The parlor's purpose was merely for casual or quick meetings, and for entertaining guests before the main event started. As such, there were no televisions or radios, only luxuriously upholstered furniture arranged around a marble-surfaced coffee table, and bookcases and oil paintings along the walls. Simple but elegant. The wallpaper in this room was of twining rose vines, a pattern that complemented the golden ivy leaves threaded into the rose-pink rug covering most of the old wooden floors. Sunlight shone through the white, gauzy curtains, though thunder boomed in the distance. A storm was brewing.

She motioned to the tray of sugar cookies and

fruit-flavored tea sitting on the coffee table. "Help yourself."

"Thanks, but I'm watching my figure." He grinned. "I thought you didn't like sweets."

"A girl can change her mind," she said, suggestively running her eyes down and up his lounging form. That cocky son of a bitch looked too damn comfortable, as if he thought he was about to own this place.

Her not-so-discreet perusal of his body also served to sharpen his gaze with lust.

Ugh. As if she'd ever consider bedding him. She'd rather jump naked into a frozen lake.

Her charming smile spoke otherwise, weaving a lie, making the enemy see what she wanted him to see and think what she wanted him to think. Just as Daddy Dearest had taught her.

Clearing his throat and loosening his tie, Strider sat forward, bracing his elbows on his knees. "I assume you brought me here for a specific purpose. It wasn't easy getting away from the summit. My Beta is capable, but I'd rather be there myself."

"A sentiment I understand all too well," she replied smoothly, keeping up the pretense of a polite smile. "I've brought you here to discuss a mating arrangement that would unite our packs for mutual gain."

His breath caught, his heart skipped a beat. She might have missed it had she not been listening so closely, gauging his reaction. Recovering, he said with nonchalance, "I thought you were taken."

"I could never bring myself to mate the man who murdered my father," she growled, a shadow of the hatred she'd felt for her future mate singeing every word. It would be easy to slip into that anger, to give in to its insatiable hunger, but she kept it in check. Never again would she allow herself to be controlled by it.

"I see," murmured Strider, eyeing the shimmering crescent moon Marking on the back of her hand. "And if all of this is so, why do you reek of him?"

A question she had anticipated. "He followed me home, under the impression he was going to mate me."

"But?"

"I tricked him. His previous Alpha fired him, told him he can't retain him since I was Marked by him. It would be against the law. With nowhere else to go, he came with me. Just like I'd planned. I needed to separate him from his allies if I was to gain his trust, which will make what I'm about to do a hell of a lot easier." She leaned forward, grinning conspiratorially. "When the time is right, I want you to help me kill him. That's the other reason I asked you to come here." She stood, gazing down at him with faked hunger in her eyes, and cozied up next to him on the opposite sofa. His eyes immediately darted to her cleavage.

Classy.

She ran a fingernail up his thigh, grazing dangerously close to his crotch. "I need a man of your expertise, Strider. A man of your vision and talent. A man who's not afraid to break some laws in order to see justice served. My father never got retribution for his murder. It's time we rectified that."

He whistled low, something akin to awe shining in his eyes. "Whoever thought noble, fierce Breanna Whiteclaw could be so delightfully vicious? I may have underestimated your character. And you've certainly underestimated mine."

The gun was pulled and pointed at her before she could blink.

CHAPTER SIXTEEN

SHADOW FORGOT HOW TO BREATHE. TIME STOPPED AS he gazed at the pistol aimed at his mate's chest. The bullet would go straight through her heart before he got within five feet of Strider.

Dammit! Why the hell was she so reckless? She'd said to trust her. But damn it if she wasn't making it nearly impossible to do so when her life was in mortal danger.

Stay back, she warned him through their bond. *I've got this.*

He's pointing a gun at you, he said brusquely, feeling the need to state the obvious since it seemed she had forgotten the danger she was in.

Let me handle it.

Shadow tensed, watching with bated breath from the peephole drilled through one of the books lining the bookcase. The books had all been secured to the shelves, which had been drilled into the wall so that when the wall swung open, you wouldn't have a mess. Shadow loved the shit out of secret passages and rooms like the one he now hid in. Breanna had assured him there were plenty more to be found throughout Bear's home. He'd wanted to have ways to escape in case the house was compromised. Too bad Bear hadn't been here when Shadow came for him. Otherwise, he might have lived to fuck people over another day.

Shadow's heart hammered the entire time he watched his mate. God, now he was calling her his mate. His mind might not be made up about her, but it seemed his heart knew what it wanted.

Breanna slowly raised both hands, not even daring to blink. Her eyes flicked to the gun and back to Strider's face. "You sure you want to do this? Think of the repercussions."

"Think of the gains," he said, smiling with that wicked gleam to his eyes Shadow didn't like one bit. "With you gone, I'll be free to swoop in and claim your pack for my own. Since you don't have any heirs to pass the crown to, it can technically go to anyone. Luckily, I've made a few alterations to your will."

"You're bluffing."

"Want to test that theory, love?"

"It's impossible. That would involve… Wait. You used magic."

"Possibly. I do have friends in high places." A sliver of fear flashed across his eyes, but it was gone before Shadow could analyze it.

Breanna set her jaw and glared at him. "Just like you've been using magic to attack my pack?"

Strider didn't move. "I don't know what you're talking about."

"I call bullshit. We found your hair and sent it off for testing. The DNA matched yours."

Shadow admired her ability to lie directly to someone's face to glean information. She would have made a fine bounty hunter. While it was true they'd sent the hair off to one of Shadow's contacts, they hadn't heard back from him yet.

Strider swallowed, paling slightly.

Breanna's breathing quickened. "It was you," she breathed. "It was you this entire time."

He continued staring at her, not saying a word. The gun in his hand had begun to shake. He hung his head low, shadowing his gaze. His voice was tight with emotion when he finally spoke. "You are an Alpha. You know what it's like trying to protect your pack, to give them the best the world has to offer while trying to keep them sheltered from the darkness. And you especially should know what it's like paying for your father's sins."

"What are you talking about?" she murmured, staring.

He growled, baring his teeth. They had lengthened, sharpened. "My father was a gambler, with an addiction to wealth. Wealth that he obtained by any means necessary. He didn't care about the pack. All he cared about was getting more money, from anyone."

"Your father fell in with bad people?" Another lure cast—Shadow had told Breanna what Orion had spilled to him during their lovely chat in the hallway back at the castle.

Strider shook his head. "My father was a good man. He really was. He started out with good intentions, but... curse him! He left us all to rot! Left me to try to clean up his colossal mess!"

"Strider, calm down—"

"I can't! They're going to kill me and my pack if I don't do this! I can't let that happen!"

He started to pull the trigger.

Breanna sucked in her last breath.

And Shadow burst from the wall as though he'd been catapulted from it, in full wolf form.

Strider startled and whipped his head around. Breanna took the opportunity to lunge for the gun.

A gunshot went off.

Shadow froze.

Breanna gasped—the bullet had grazed her arm, which had begun to bleed.

The scent of her blood filled the air and met Shadow's nose.

That son of a bitch had just shot his mate.

With an outraged snarl, he leaped for the couch, having every intention of tearing that bastard's head clean off.

Strider swore, dropped the gun, and dove out of the way as Shadow slammed into the cushions.

Snarling, Strider tore his shirt clean off and Shifted into a golden wolf. The two wolves rushed at each other, biting, clawing, and growling. They rolled along the floor, crashed into furniture, slammed against walls, knocked bookcases down.

Breanna watched, heart pounding. What to do, what

to do, what to do—

With expert efficiency, she checked the magazine of the gun. Fully loaded, save for the bullet that had kissed her arm. Sliding the magazine back into place, she aimed.

They were moving so fast... What if she clipped Shadow or worse?

Shadow, she said through their bond, *I need a clear shot.*

That makes two of us, cupcake. He went to step backward, his paw landing on a tipped-over vase. It went sliding across the room, taking his balance with it and making him stumble.

Strider didn't waste any time. Shadow yelped as the golden wolf bit his throat, making to tear it.

It was now or never.

Sending up a quick prayer and never taking her eyes off her mate, Breanna fired.

The gunshot seemed to echo. Time slowed as the bullet left the chamber and sailed across the room. It embedded itself in Strider's leg. His head tipped back as he yowled in pain.

Breanna took her chance. She Shifted, turning into a wolf the color of smoke, and ran for Strider. Her teeth sank into his injured leg, and she yanked him off her mate.

Following another pained whine, he whirled on her, eyes full of rage.

Oh, she would show him rage. And no mercy.

This was the man who'd tried to kill her, her mate, and her pack, had tried taking away what had belonged to her family for generations. She would be damned if she'd let him get away without a few scrapes.

The two wolves fought hard and dirty. Strider was all muscle with no technique, whereas Breanna's father had taught her not only how to fight as a human but as a wolf, as well. It really wasn't a fair contest. Shadow pawed at the floor, whining to join her, but she told him to stay back. She could handle this. She would do what any Alpha had to—defend the honor and interests of her pack.

Though she may be in a fight to the death, for the first time in her life she did not question her ability or right to be a queen of wolves.

Shadow's strength poured through their bond.

Strider's movements were slowing as the injury drained his energy.

Good. Time to end this.

The battle only served to wake her up, to give her a much-needed adrenaline boost. Every sense was sharp; no movement of her enemy's went unnoticed. Sensing his imminent defeat, Strider turned for the door. Breanna lunged—and drove the two of them straight through the window.

Glass gave way beneath the force of their flying bodies, shattering and raining down on them as they landed on the grass outside.

Guards startled. Breanna landed on top of Strider, jaws open and locked around his throat. With a warning growl, she bit and began to twist, tearing flesh—

Strider abruptly Shifted back to his human form, his skin covered in sweat and very pale. "Okay, okay!" he shrieked. "I surrender! Fuck, don't kill me!"

Breanna Changed back, standing and planting her foot on his throat. She rattled off the attacks on her pack. "Do you confess to these crimes?"

"Yes! Yes! Let me go!"

She smiled, wicked and beautiful. "Gladly." He never saw her fist coming. Clipping his temple, she knocked him out cold. She panted hard, her gaze lingering on Strider before looking at the rest of her pack. Shadow, now human again, had joined them on the lawn. He gazed at her with such immense pride, she thought her knees would give out.

Her sharp eyes met Mrs. Wheaton's tawny gaze. "Why didn't your guards come to our aid when you heard the first gunshot?"

"Because we needed to see if you had what it took to really lead this pack," she said without hesitation, stepping forward. "But most of all, you needed to prove to yourself that you could, that you were every bit as strong as Bear." She glanced at Strider and back to Breanna, placing a fist over her heart. "It appears we were right—you've had it in you all along, the capacity to be a strong and great queen. You just needed to see it for yourself to believe it." She knelt on one knee in the grass, as did all the other guards and gathered pack members.

Her heart soared as she looked around, hardly able to believe what she was seeing. Grinning, she looked at Shadow.

And he smiled back.

CHAPTER SEVENTEEN

KAILEY NOTICED THE WOMAN WHO HAD JUST BEEN seated in her section right away. Hell, with her looks, practically everyone in the diner had noticed her. How could they not? Her clothing, hair, and makeup, even the way she delicately sipped her coffee, screamed that she came from money. She had a hypnotic beauty about her that made it difficult to look away. Long blond hair, wide, brilliant-blue eyes framed in thick, ebony lashes, perfectly smooth porcelain skin, and full lips the color of fresh blood.

As if she'd sensed her staring, the woman's eyes flicked to Kailey's. Blinking rapidly, Kailey quickly looked away and smoothed her apron. Feeling her cheeks heat, she snatched up the next order and tried not to trip as she delivered it to the hungry patrons.

"Sorry about the wait," she said to the elderly couple, tacking on a smile for good measure. "Is there anything else I can get for you?"

"No, dear," said the woman, glancing around Kailey with a frown. "But that woman over there has been staring at you. Perhaps she needs something?"

Kailey's spine went rigid. She knew exactly whom they were talking about. Clearing her throat, she smiled again. "I'll see what, um, she needs. Thank you."

For some reason, her heart started pounding as she approached the woman. Her palms slicked, and her stomach tumbled with nerves.

Startled, she realized she was afraid of this beautiful stranger. There was a predatory gleam in her eyes, as though Kailey were a cockroach she couldn't wait to squish beneath her designer pumps.

Kailey's mouth went dry as she stopped beside the table. The only sensation she was aware of was the pounding of her heart; she wasn't even sure she was breathing.

She opened her mouth to speak, but no words would come out. Went to draw breath, but none would come.

Panic began to set in as her lungs started to burn. Oh God! Was she choking? She hadn't been chewing on anything.

What's happening? her frantic mind screamed as she desperately tried to inhale but couldn't seem to find the air. It was as if all the oxygen in the room had been sucked out.

All the while the woman continued to watch unblinkingly with that eerie, cat-like smile.

All at once sweet air rushed down Kailey's throat and into her lungs. Gasping, she choked on the sudden intake of air and went into a coughing fit. She turned her head to cough on her sleeve as patrons turned to stare.

"Are you all right?" the woman asked in a voice dark as night. Faint disgust made her crimson lips stiffen. "I do hope you're not diseased."

Diseased, not sick. Like vermin.

"No, ma'am, I'm not sick," Kailey rasped. "Just had something caught in my throat."

The woman raised a brow, looking annoyed. "I've been waiting for over five minutes for more coffee."

Kailey glanced at her cup. It wasn't even half empty. Her teeth gritted in irritation. So she was going to be one of those patrons. "I apologize, ma'am. I'll get you a pot."

"No," the woman said sharply as Kailey started to walk away. "You'll pour it for me, whenever I motion for you. I don't pour my own coffee."

It took extreme effort not to raise a brow. Not trusting herself not to rattle off some smartass comment, Kailey swiftly walked away, trying to ignore the fact that her palms were still sweating and her heart still racing.

A tall, handsome man dressed in a mustard-yellow peacoat, an indigo scarf, and khaki-colored dress slacks walked in. All movement in the restaurant ceased as head after head turned to stare as he walked toward the booth with the elegant woman and sat down.

She didn't even look up from her phone. "You're late," she said tersely.

"I had some unexpected business to attend to," he said, smiling pleasantly. A trio of young women walked by, grinning at him and whispering to each other.

He smiled back.

"Ugh," the woman said with a shiver. "How you can stand to live among humans, let alone flirt with them, is beyond me."

"They have their charms," he said, casting one last lingering glance at the girls. "Shall we discuss business?"

A skinny brunette timidly approached the table. "I expect this to be fresh," the woman said as Kailey started to pour the steaming coffee into her cup. "No, no! 'Fresh' means I want a new cup."

Pursing her lips, Kailey took the cup and stalked off.

The woman growled and massaged her temples. "Humans are so barbaric. It gives me chills thinking about the germs crawling on my skin just from breathing this air."

"It was an inconspicuous place to meet," the man said affably. "And their chicken potpie is quite good."

That made her nearly gag.

Kailey returned with a fresh cup filled with coffee. "Is there anything else I can—"

"Leave us," the woman snapped, not deigning to look at Kailey.

The waitress's face turned red, and her hands balled into fists.

"Actually, love," the man said, flashing her a dashing smile, "I would like your chicken potpie and garden salad special."

She seemed to cheer right up under his attention. "Of course, sir. I'll get that in right away."

He looked at the woman smugly as the waitress

scampered away. "Is it really so hard for you to be nice?"

"Don't test me, Nigel. Being around these people, these savages, is nearly unbearable. Were you able to get to Strider before the DPI could question him?"

"Indeed, Mistress. One of the cops on my payroll let me slip into his interrogation room, posing as a detective. No one suspected a thing."

"You're sure he won't remember anything about my involvement in the Whiteclaw Pack attacks?"

"You do realize whom you're talking to, don't you? My memory-erasing skills are second to none."

Kailey delivered the chicken potpie and salad combo, smiling shyly at Nigel, who was all too happy to smile right back. He cast a suggestive glance down her backside as she walked back to the counter.

"This is disgusting," the woman said, sipping her coffee. "I can hardly stand to drink this. Even made fresh, it's vile. Don't humans know how to make decent coffee?"

"Well, not everyone can afford private five-star chefs who can make everything from scratch for you," Nigel said wryly, digging into his pie. "How go your conquests?"

"Attaining the Whiteclaw Pack was a disaster, thanks to that bumbling idiot, Strider. I truly thought he had some potential to join the Order, but clearly I was wrong. Having the wealth of the Whiteclaw Pack, and all those werewolves at my disposal, would have been nice. Oh well. No sense fussing over it now. At least my other... business ventures have gone well."

"You look like you have more color in you, dyed hair aside," he said with a grin. "What's this alias?"

"Melaney," she said with a flourish. "A mysterious witch with an even more mysterious, wealthy employer."

"Well, at least you're consistent. 'Melaney' and 'Mistress Black' both start with the letter M."

"Keep your voice down!"

"Why? I don't sense any other paranormals in here. And no one's spying on us—I've already bewitched the place to ward off eavesdropping spells. Thus, another reason for us to meet here. Besides, it's not as if these humans are going to know what we're talking about." Sensing her irritation, he decided to change the subject. "I take it soul-collecting is going well?"

"Quite. With me stealing the life from paranormal creatures all over the country, no one has been able to connect the dots just yet. They'll never see me coming until it's too late."

Nigel shivered under the power-hungry, dark look in her eyes. "Glad to hear it," he said, pasting on a smile. Sometimes he wondered just what kind of monster he was helping to unleash by aiding Mistress Black, but he couldn't afford not to, not now. He was in too deep.

He quickly finished his pie and salad, eager to be away from the woman he both desired and feared. Kailey brought the check, which Nigel insisted on paying. He left her a generous tip.

Melaney, or rather, Mistress Black, watched the way his eyes followed Kailey. He genuinely liked this girl. Which was absurd, with her sitting in front of him. Why ogle a common human when he could have a goddess? It was insulting. At one point she might have considered bedding him. He was handsome, powerful, and rich enough. But his troublesome preference for human companionship was a deal-breaker. There was no telling what foul diseases he'd caught.

Still didn't mean she couldn't have a little more fun...

With a flick of her wrist, Kailey's shoelaces tied themselves together, making her trip. She pitched forward, dropping Nigel's empty plates and Melaney's mostly empty coffee cup. Kailey's face flared bright red as a waiter rushed to help her.

Nigel's jaw ticked. "Did you really have to trip her?"

"That's nothing. You should have seen the look of terror on her face earlier when I choked her."

He stared at her, silent. And slightly pale. "You revel in people's fear of you, don't you?"

She stared at Kailey as she untied her shoes, looking incredibly puzzled, while the waiter picked up her mess. "If you'd spent most of your childhood and adult life living in fear, you'd become addicted to people fearing you, too." She rose. "I must be going. Pleasure doing business with you, as always. I'll call on you if I'm in need of your services again."

He made himself grasp her hand and kiss the back of it. "The pleasure is all mine."

She gripped his hand, squeezing hard while searching his eyes. Taking a step closer, she whispered, "If you ever think of turning me in, I'll hunt you down myself and kill you. Oh, don't look surprised, love. I can sense your fear, your uncertainty. This is the right path, what I'm trying to do. All this violence, all this bloodshed, will be worth it someday when our kind can at last live in a world free from persecution. We will be free to be what we were meant to be without fear of retribution." At last she released his hand. It was bright red. He shook it out, frowning.

She smiled. "You'll thank me someday." Patting his chest, she sauntered off to the waiting limo outside.

From behind the counter, Kailey stood shaking, watching the woman leave. She wasn't a clumsy person… and her shoes! How on earth had they tied themselves together? *That woman is responsible,* her subconscious whispered, however irrational it sounded.

The driver opened the car door, waiting for the woman to get inside.

As if sensing her watching, the woman looked over her shoulder and locked eyes with Kailey. Smiling, she waved her hand over her face. Her skin and hair shimmered for a moment. The blond hair turned a rich, deep brown, but her eyes were the same—that striking, rich blue that reminded her of the deep ocean. The features of her face changed slightly, becoming sharper and yet more striking for it. If it weren't for her eye color, Kailey might think her to be an entirely different woman.

With a wink, she got in the car.

The tray of dirty plates and glasses Kailey had been holding slipped from her fingers, crashing onto the floor.

CHAPTER EIGHTEEN

"WHAT DO YOU MEAN HE DOESN'T REMEMBER?" Breanna asked, pacing the room.

Shadow and Breanna stood in her bedroom, dressed in the white ceremonial robes of the mating couple. It was the night of the full moon, the evening the two of them must mate or be doomed never to fall in love ever again. The ceremony was to take place within ten minutes. Their witnesses had already gathered outside the door, awaiting the clock to strike the hour. Outside, the moon hung low in the sky. Actually, it might have been higher up than it appeared. It was just so *big* tonight, a swollen sphere with a red tinge to it and a crimson halo.

Shadow still couldn't believe the mating ceremony was here, that they were actually going through with it. If someone had asked him if they'd mate when he'd first Marked Breanna, he would have said, "Hell, no!"

For once, he was happy to be wrong.

Now, if he could just calm down his mate.

Jack's delivery of the bad news regarding Strider couldn't have been more ill timed, but Shadow supposed it couldn't be helped. They were Alphas, after all. Pack business couldn't wait for a convenient time, especially a revelation this big.

Jack stood just inside the doorway, shifting his weight as his frown became more severe. "The DPI thinks some kind of memory-erasing spell was activated recently, sometime shortly after they booked him. He doesn't remember anything about attacking the Whiteclaw Pack or even how he got to our territory."

Breanna swore.

Shadow's eyes narrowed. "So are they, what, going to let him go?"

"No. That's actually the good news. He was scared shitless and ended up confessing to the murder of his former mate. Plus, they have the footage of him pulling a gun on Breanna from that hidden camera in the parlor. Bastard will be lucky if he ever sees the light of day again for that shit."

Shadow nodded. "Good. That prick doesn't deserve to walk free, not after what he's done. At least justice will be served for someone. Not to mention his pack will be taken care of by a good leader now." Shortly after news spread of Strider's sentencing, the pack unanimously voted one of their own to be the new Alpha—a senior member with morals and integrity. "Plus, now they're protected from the mobsters thanks to some high-level friends in the DPI and witching community."

That was good news. The first thing Breanna had thought about after the trial was what would become of Strider's pack, but now she saw she had nothing to worry about.

Jack left shortly thereafter, promising to see them in a moment. That was going to be awkward as hell, Shadow making love to Jack's former crush right in front of him. But it couldn't be helped, even though he would rather consummate their union in private. All royal werewolf pairings had to be "witnessed," much like human monarchies of old.

Shadow reached for Breanna's hand and pulled her to him. "You okay?" he murmured.

She stood there staring at his chest, breathing hard. "I don't know. Yes and no, I suppose. On one hand, I'm glad he'll be going to jail forever. On the other, I wish it was partly because of what he's done to try to sabotage my pack's well-being."

He kissed her forehead and folded her against his chest, holding her. "It'll be all right. It's over now. You're safe. Your pack is safe." He lifted her chin to stare into her beautiful eyes. "And we have each other."

Her worry fell away, molding into a radiant smile. "Soon, forever."

A knock came at the door.

It was time.

Only Breanna's council, consisting of five members, was present to witness the mating ceremony, with Jack officiating. He'd insisted as not only Breanna's Beta, but also as her friend. His smile at Shadow as he read the binding contract made her believe maybe the two of them could someday find their way to friendship, as well.

His clenched jaw as they proceeded to the mating bed, however, spoke otherwise.

At Breanna's insistence, they'd drawn the thick canopy shut, providing some meager form of privacy. Shadow and Breanna sat on their knees at the center of the bed, facing each other.

Their packmates began fervently chanting the words that would activate the binding spell.

Her heart pounded, her breath coming in faster and faster.

"You ready?" Shadow murmured, stroking her cheek with his knuckles.

Would she ever be ready to bind herself to someone forever? No. Not this independent spirit. But would she for her pack's safety and well-being? Absolutely.

She nodded.

He leaned in and kissed her tenderly, questioningly.

You lead, he said through their bond.

Her nerves melted away. Being in control was something she was born to do. He must have sensed that it would help her if she led them through this, giving her something else to focus on other than the watchful eyes surrounding them.

Her heart clenched out of gratitude. Kissing him deeply, she shrugged out of her robe as he did the same, leaving them both naked. Her mouth crushed his as she tipped them backward against the satin pillows.

A multitude of candles washed the room in soft light. Their shadows danced along the walls as they kissed. Breanna's inner Alpha took charge, eager to finally lay with its mate. Her loins ached, especially as Shadow's fingers reached inside her while his thumb stroked her throbbing sex.

She moaned, her back arching.

"You're ready for me," he whispered into her ear, catching her earlobe between his teeth.

Her breathing was ragged now, her nipples rubbing against his chest as she rocked her hips. Her sex ground against his hardened cock as it replaced his hand, not quite going in but rather teasing her.

Shadow's hands clenched the sheets. He watched her, staring into her eyes, almost begging her with his gaze to take him.

She gripped his cock, angling it upward—then slid him inside of her.

He groaned low as she rode him, sitting upright and letting her body take over. He gripped her thighs, spreading her legs wider. She cried out as he pierced her core, delivering wave after wave of white-hot pleasure. She fell forward, kissing him as though his mouth were water and she hadn't had anything to drink in days.

He broke the barrage of kisses to take one of her breasts in his mouth and tease the nipple with his masterful tongue.

She bucked more desperately, whimpering. He gripped her rear, driving himself harder, faster, deeper—

The air lit up with vivid blue light about the same time they came, the wave of their orgasms rising and falling as one.

When the light faded away, swirling indigo tattoos of crescent moons, clouds, and stars curled along their upper backs, shoulders, arms, and chests.

The room cheered, but Breanna barely saw or heard what else was going on around her.

Her eyes were only on Shadow—her new mate.

She wrapped her arms around him as they sat up, and she smiled. "Looks like you're stuck with me, for better or for worse."

He grinned, a dreamy look on his face. "For better. Always for better."

He kissed her. And she couldn't think of a time in her life she'd been happier.

At last, they each had a family again.

They were home.

THE END

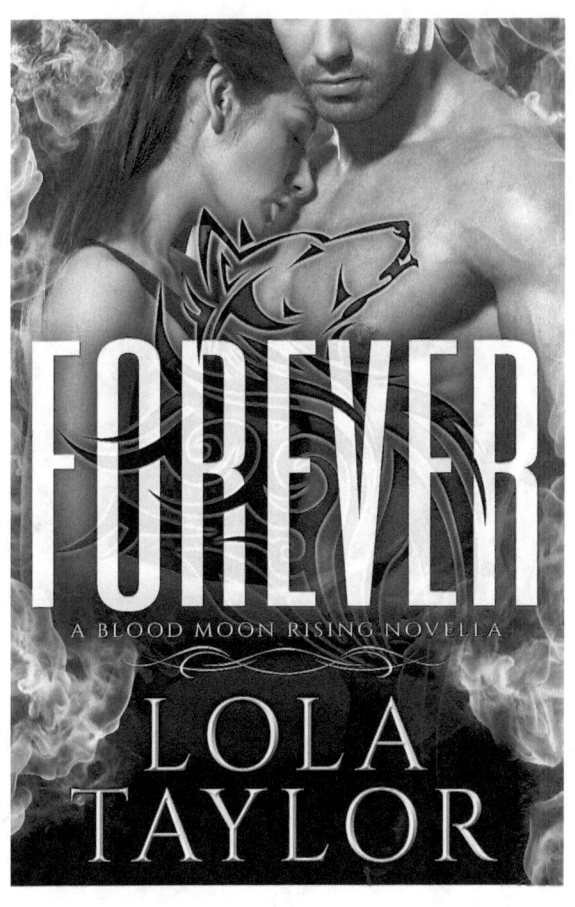

Shadow and Breanna's story continues in *Forever,* coming soon.
Visit www.lolataylorbooks.com to sign up for new release notifications.

OTHER BOOKS BY
LOLA TAYLOR

The Her Dark Desires Trilogy
Carnal (free for a limited time!)
Sinful
Soulful (coming soon!)

Blood Moon Rising
Fever (free for a limited time!)
Protector
Betrayal
Captured
Sacrifice
Ritual

Blood Moon Rising companion novels
Lust
Forever (coming soon!)

Standalone novels
Shatter

For a full list of titles, please visit
www.lolataylorbooks.com.

Your opinion matters—please leave a review!

Thank you for reading my book! If you have a moment, I'd really appreciate an honest rating and review. They help authors stand out in a busy marketplace, plus they give browsing readers the nitty-gritty on books they're shopping. Everyone wins when you rate and review, so please do! Your opinion counts!

ABOUT THE AUTHOR

"Lola Taylor" is a pen name created for the romances I can't show my grandma without blushing. My favorite genre to write is romantic suspense, usually involving hot werewolves, warlocks, or any other type of paranormal creature. Keep the action hot and the romance hotter—that's my motto! I'm a horror film junkie, I still love Halloween as an adult (seriously, I think I get more excited for it than some kids do), and what precious spare time

I have is spent with my family, reading (everything from sci fi to middle grade), playing the flute, painting pretty pictures, or screwing around on Pinterest or Etsy. Hailing from the South, I currently live in the Midwest with five fur babies and my hubby.

You can connect with me on Facebook (www.facebook.com/lolataylorbooks) or my email (lolawritespnr@gmail.com). Learn more about me and my books at www.lolataylorbooks.com.